Death of Mr. Agarwal

I0555447

Zaid Mannu

WORDIT ART FUND

This book has been fully funded by the Wordit Art Fund. Wordit Art Fund
helps deserving authors publish their work by providing monetary
support. To apply for funding, please visit us at
www.BecomeShakespeare.com

First published in 2017 by

Becomeshakespeare.com
Wordit Content Design & Editing Services Pvt Ltd
Unit - 26, Building A-1, Nr Wadala RTO, Wadala (East),
Mumbai 400037, India
T:+91 8080226699

©
ISBN 978-93-86487-43-8

DEDICATION

To the writers, may you find the words you are looking for.

To the travelers, may the wind be in your sails

To the thinkers, may your thoughts never stump you.

To the lovers, may you be brave enough to love again.

And to the warriors, may the force be with you.

Death of Mr. Agarwal

ACKNOWLEDGMENTS

To my parents, thanks for the incredible support, nothing would be possible without you.

To my sisters, thanks for being there, there is truly no one like you both.

To my little niece Taisha, it is a joy to have you in my life.

To my Friends, thanks for all the love.

To the rest of my family, thanks for constant support.

Furthermore I would like to thank Prarthana Dixit for the amazing cover design.

CONTENTS

CHAPTER ONE

The phone was ringing for what seemed like hours. Ayaan
was in his bed in between a deep sleep when the phone
started to ring for the first time. He woke up after the fourth
ring and decided against picking it up. He was asleep on the
far left of the bed and his phone was plugged in to a port on
the dresser table which was situated on the right of the bed.
It took the phone quite some time to convince Ayaan to slide
over to the other side of the bed and finally pick up the
phone. Somehow he remembered exactly where he placed
his mobile phone on the dresser when he went to sleep.
Sleep was such an easy thing to get, he could just shut his
eyes and slide over to the other side of the bed and he will be
fast asleep in no time, Ayaan was sure. However he resisted
his urge to sleep and he had to fight very hard to do so. With
his eyes shut he picked up the phone.

"Sir! Sir! Ayaan sir! We have got a case".

For a second, Ayaan was confused as he didn't realize
what was going on. He could barely open his eyes and after
much of struggle he managed to open his left eye. It seemed
ages had passed since he had slept and he was ready to sleep
for a couple more. He checked the digital clock on the
dresser next to the bed, the same place where he had picked
up his phone. The display on the clock said 47. Ayaan

considered that for a moment and then managed to open his right eye too, and then he saw what the clock actually read. He then brought his phone into his vision, the call was still active and the caller ID read "Milan".

Pieces seem to be falling into place now for Ayaan, as he raised the phone to his right ear.

"it's 4 o clock Milan, what do you want?"

"We have got a case sir Ayaan sir, a very important case"

He realized that he had already been told that before, but he still didn't think that was enough to justify the hindrance.

"Couldn't it wait till the morning, what's so important about this case?" Ayaan asked irritated.

"No sir, I am afraid it can't sir, its Mr. Agarwal, he is dead..... I mean murdered sir".

"I don't know any Mr. Agarwal"

"He is..... I mean was the owner of Agarwal Traders sir"

"What is Agarwal Traders.....? Who is Mr. Agarwal....? Why am I being bothered? You know very well Milan I don't take cases without references"

"I know sir", Milan replied, "But commissioner Vishnu asked for you specifically".

"Well then ask Commissioner Vishnu to appoint some of his lousy, no good, suck up inspectors for this case".

Ayaan didn't mean that at all, and as there was no solid response from the other end of the call he realized Milan didn't agree to the idea too. But at this moment Ayaan could have confessed for the murder of Mr. Agarkar himself if it would just allow him to go back to sleep again.

"But he insisted" said Milan from the other end of the phone after an awfully long pause.
Ayaan realized that there was no getting out of it, so he decided to concur.

"Alright, where?"

"Olympus building" said the voice of a delighted man.

"Okay, I will see you there" replied Ayaan exhausted.

Even after he put his phone away, Ayaan Shahi stayed in bed for some time, blank in thought and expression, just too lazy for... Pretty much everything. Finally he gathered up the strength to get his feet on the mat adjacent to his bed, he lifted his upper body next and tried to balance it above his wobbly legs. After recapturing the ability to stand erect, Ayaan turned his head to have a look at the clock on his dresser, it read 4:56. Ayaan had trouble believing that only 9 minutes had passed, it seemed like hours. He walked towards the bathroom door and opened it, turned on the lights which gave his eyes near blindness for a second. He next took his toothbrush from the holder and put some toothpaste on it which was right next to it. He started brushing, and then looked up in the mirror. The Ayaan in the mirror had a shabby, uncombed hair, thick and scruffy beard and mouth filled with white paste. He scrubbed his beard with his hand

11

I got to shave, he concluded

Shaving came later though he had to do a couple of things before that, he finished brushing his teeth, gargled, spat out the foamy water and the relieved himself on the toilet seat. When he had concluded his business there he walked in the shower and had a nice and clean bath. The water was warm and the right amount of warm. The exact kind that is needed to wake up a man after a half night sleep. After the bath he shaved.

While he was shaving Ayaan saw his father in the mirror, smiling through his thick beard, the kind Ayaan had just shaved but a little longer. His father had a beard chest long. He was staring at Ayaan with his black eyes, glaring. Ayaan splashed cold water on his face and looked again. Ayaan knew himself very well, and lately he had been missing his father a lot. Probably because this was the month when the disease was first detected. He didn't even want to think what happened afterwards, it made him furious and so he decided to not think about it at the moment, he had much more important things to deal with than dwelling in the past. He stepped out of the bathroom wiped himself dry and put on a new clothes. He selected a black shirt and jeans. Although he preferred wearing white, but with murder scenes it was always tricky. He turned to see the clock on the dresser again, it read 5:21. Ayaan realized that it was time for his morning prayer and decided to attend to it.

He took out a sheet of cloth spread it on the floor in the appropriate direction and raised his arms to his ears and lost himself. He wasn't found until he concluded his prayers and asked God for wisdom, as he would require it very much for his case to come. He prayed for his mother, his wife...his beautiful wife and his father.... Especially his father, whom he missed the most these days. It took him several minutes to get his phone, wallet and his briefcase which he carried with him to his every case. He also took his business card from the top drawer in his dresser, it was a blue colored card with his contact details, and it read Ayaan Shahi, private investigator. He opened his room door and walked into the hallway. It was silent as was expected at 5 in the morning; he opened the room door next to his room. Although the air conditioner was making awfully loud noise, his little daughter was fast asleep under a blanket. He closed the door and went to the living room. To his left was the dining table and upon it lay a fruit basket. Ayaan was famished, so he walked over to have a look. There were three apples, one orange and a rotten banana. He took the apple and took a huge bite, it was juicy and fresh, and the apple juice ran down his lips to his chin. He wiped it with the sleeve of his shirt and continued to quell his hunger. He heard a door creek open behind his back, so he turned, and there stood a woman in her 30s who seemed to have woken up from a deep sleep.

"Do you need anything Ayaan sahib?" She asked politely.

It was Salma, his live in housemaid. She was probably wondering why he was up so early and where he was about to go, but it wasn't her place to ask that to him.

"No nothing, I have to leave for work and I will be gone for a couple of hours"

"Oh that's fine"
Ayaan took another Apple from the basket and took his briefcase, ready to leave. Salma was on her way to her room.
"Salma" Ayaan called out, she stopped and turned.

"Make sure you have Ayman ready for school, before I get home, I don't want her to be late."

"I will" she replied courteously, and returned to her room. Today Ayaan would have to drop his daughter to school, as there was a transport strike in the city and no busses or rickshaws would be available, he recalled.

He took his car keys grabbed his essentials and walked out of the apartment. He tried to think of he knew the name Milan had mentioned, or anything about the company, but nothing came to mind. He wondered what this murder case would be like, in his career as a private investigator, he had come across variety of murder cases, some were simple like a case of a husband strangling his wife to death, but some were horrific and gruesome and simply made him nauseous. He hoped for challenge but prayed for it to be nothing more than a bullet in the head. Ayaan halted, he had forgotten something, something very important. He turned, opened his apartment door and walked straight into his room. He went towards his closet and opened it. There were three drawers in the closet, one had his ties and another had his under garments. He opened the third drawer.

He took out his 9mm handgun and also the holster next to it. He checked if it was loaded, which it was and put it into a holster which he then attached to his belt. Now Ayaan was ready.

CHAPTER TWO

It took Ayaan precisely 10 minutes to get to the parking of the building. This was because he waited for an elevator that never came, probably because some idiotic person left the door of the elevator open on some floor. So Ayaan had to climb down 5 flights of stairs to get down. It wasn't at all a waste of time, he got to finish another one of his apples and also got to stretch his legs a bit. It seemed like a necessary warm up for his body and mind. He found his parked car. He owned a white sedan, which was very powerful and luxurious no doubt, but what was intriguing is that the Germans called it "the people's car" which was hard to believe because it fit five people with utmost difficulty. But the roads of this country made off-roading a joy ride, so luxury and comfort were a priority.

Ayaan had the car cleaned yesterday evening so it was tidy and sparkly to look at. Ayaan got in the driver's seat, started the engine and drove out on to the road. The sun was rising on the left hand side and it was an incredible view. The view was complimented with the lack of traffic, which made it a pleasant ride. Olympus building wasn't very far away do it took Ayaan only 10 minutes to reach it. As he was about to reach he checked his watch on his left hand, it read 6:05. The building came into view on an empty street, Ayaan grabbed his phone and was about to call Milan, when he saw man rapidly waving his hands below the Olympus building. It was Milan. A short man nearly 4 inches shorter than Ayaan and really plump. He was kind of a man who you would still call cute, and not in a flirting way but in a childish, immature way. He was young too, only 24 years and really passionate about his work. He had been working with Ayaan for over 2 years now and Ayaan had come to like him very much. He was really fond of the boy's work and his commitment towards it. He was sweet and polite as well, until you called him by his first name. Chetak Milan was what his father named him. Umesh Milan, a sub inspector who climbed up to the ladder to being a sub inspector without corruption or bribery. He had never given or accepted bribes, and after his years of hard earned pay, he bought himself a scooter named Chetak, which he cherished. So after he was blessed with his one and only son whom he loved truly, he named him after the other thing he loved truly in this world.

Ayaan parked his car and got out of it. He walked towards Milan who was on the other side of the street, standing in front of a glass building. The entire street was filled with office buildings and Olympus was probably the most appealing. Ayaan had crossed this street numerous times, but he had never had any reason to stop and loiter around. Probably because there were hardly any criminal cases in this area. This was considered to be one of the safest areas in the city, Ayaan was used to visiting areas with an infamous reputation. Ayaan got closer the building, it was a complete glass structure, with 9 floors... Could have been 10 hard to say. Ayaan never really cared for contemporary architecture, especially for an office building. Why would anyone be bothered about the exterior of a building when people who work there hardly get to see it. It was an absolute waste of money. Plus the building adjacent to the glass building was so old that it looked like it was built before the invention of glass. Ayaan reached where Milan was standing.

"Sir... Good morning sir", he greeted. Ayaan greeted him in return.

"So what have we got here".

"A simple case sir, a one bullet kill".

"Aha!" Ayaan exclaimed, he checked his holster to make sure he had his gun. It was intact, which relived Ayaan a little.

"Anything else" he inquired.

"No sir, nothing, the night guard went for his routine stroll and found Mr. Agarwal dead in his office, he notified the officials... And... And here we are" Milan replied.

"Very well let's go upstairs and check it out" Ayaan started walking, Milan followed.

The door were made of glass as well and they were automatic. The doors opened sideways, but when they were closed they had a picture of an earth posted on them and there was something written underneath it as well. It read "you are entering a different world". Ayaan saw the irony in the saying, but chose against commenting on it. He didn't want to speak ill of the deceased, and plus he didn't even know the victim, not even his first name, he didn't want to judge him on what he was trying to create. A better working environment perhaps, or probably something to help society, clearly that didn't sit well with others. Now all he had was a bullet in his body and death certificate.

They went into the elevator, and Milan pressed for the 3rd floor. Ayaan realized that the building did only have 9 floors, as the 9th floor was the last stop for the elevator. The elevator went up three floors and its doors slid open. The floor was surrounded by cubicles, which were probably where the employees sat and worked. Behind those dozens of cubicles, there was an office. It was made of glass but the glass was tinted so no one could see it from this side.

"Is this his office?" Ayaan guessed.

"Yes "Milan replied, "the body is inside, untouched"

Ayaan walked towards the office, opened the fancy wooden door and entered.

He saw the body, sitting comfortably on a leather seat, mouth slightly open and eyes firmly shut. Mr. Agarwal was wearing a suit and a tie and the bullet wound was on the left side of his chest. The killer clearly aimed directly for the heart. The chair Mr. Agarwal was sitting on.... Well not as much sitting as resting on was facing a wooden desk. On the left of the desk were files and papers and on the right was a coffee mug and a fancy pen. Ayaan placed his briefcase on the floor, opened it and took out a pair of gloves. After he had put on his gloves he asked Milan to do the same, and he obeyed.

His job as a private investigator was pretty simple, he had to investigate the crime scene, interrogate suspects and witnesses and with evidence prove the culprit. He then had to ask the police to arrest the offender and get money for his service to the police. As a private investigator he was not permitted to make arrests. However private investigators aren't highly respected, but Ayaan was different. In his eight years as a private investigator he had solved 29 cases. 7 of them were murder cases and others involved kidnappings, threats and others. He had worked for both individuals and for the state police and he preferred individuals any day of the week. Ayaan decided to put his thoughts about the city police aside and concentrate on the situation at hand

Mr. Agarwal was fair skinned, was bald and clean shaved. By the looks of it he looked in his late fifties, a very young age to die, Ayaan realized. He went to his desk chair and moved it to have a better look at the body. He asked Milan to take notes of the first inspection of the crime scene, as the notes would help him later if it was necessary. Although right now the case seemed pretty straight forward.

"The bullet wound is located on the left chest, seems like it nearly missed the heart" Ayaan dictated as Milan was writing down the notes.

"Judging by the penetration, the bullet was fired from less than six feet, probably from right across the desk, the killer was most likely a rookie, to miss a shot so close."

"Nevertheless" he continued, "the COD was definitely excessive blood loss, the victim could have survived if he was given immediate medical attention, but nonetheless that didn't happen, it was a slow death" he finished. He looked at Milan and he was still scribbling in a little notepad.
After he was done, he looked at Ayaan.

"Ugh! What a cruel way to go, I would have just asked for another bullet in the head, get it over with you know?" said Milan

Ayaan went back to examine the wound. "that's not entirely true" Ayaan replied. He was no stranger to near death experiences that was the reason he carried a pistol nowadays, to avoid anymore said experiences.

"Why not" asked Milan.

"Because when you are actually ready to die and have accepted the inevitable, you need time. Time to have your life flash in front of your eyes, have a last glimpse of what you are going to leave behind"

"But what about the pain".

"You can almost live with the pain, and since you have so less amount of time to live it doesn't matter about the pain. What really matters is the final closure you get for a life you lived" Ayaan finished.

Milan was probably staring at Ayaan, but he didn't care for that, he was currently focusing on the murdered victim.

"Do you think someone can live on in this world after being dead, you know kind of like 50/50, half alive, and half not so much" Milan asked in an inquisitive tone.

Ayaan chuckled, which was a weird thing to do as he had a dead body lying in front of him.

"There are only two kinds of people in this world, one are alive and others are dead, there is no middle ground."

Milan didn't say anything, he just nodded and got back to his notes.
Ayaan continues his search of the body, he had checked almost all the pockets and had found nothing. Not even a driving license or any identification. If the body had been

dumped in the river it would have been an awfully tedious task to determine this man's identity, Ayaan realized. Not that he knew a lot anyway, Ayaan didn't even know the first name of the victim, but that was just a matter of time, he knew. At least he checked the left breast pocket that was on the inside of the coat Mr. Agarwal was wearing. He felt something inside and defied to investigate it. The pocket was damp with blood and had a hole, which was the size of a bullet. Clearly the bullet had penetrated the pocket and the victim's body. He put his two fingers inside the pocket and pulled out a folded yellowish parchment with blood stains on it. Ayaan unfolded it to discover that it wasn't blank, there was a quite some text written on it, which seemed like a story.

The parchment was perfectly preserved, even though it seemed that bullet should have penetrated the paper. There was only one logical explanation and it was an important one. The title read "the pious drunkard and fornicator"

Ayaan put the parchment aside, he will have to read it later.

Milan informed him that he had already called the manager and some other important employees, to interrogate.

They had to wait for fifteen minutes before 4 people in formal shirts and pants entered the room. In the meantime Ayaan had asked Milan to interrogate the watchman, who was very shaken up about the whole incident. However, this didn't yield any information other than what they already knew.

The four people were all men, and one of them appeared to be younger than his other three colleagues. Nevertheless he was dressed in the same manner the other three were. They all came to Ayaan one by one and introduced themselves. All of them were managers. The first one to introduce himself was the advertising and marketing manager, Praveen Gandhi. He was a middle aged man with a thick mustache and black hair, which were without a doubt the result of a good dyeing. Second came Aadarsh Nayar, who was the operations manager, he was partially bald, and looked around the same age as Mr. Agarwal. The other two, Mohit and Fravash were assistant managers to the other two. They were both young, but Mohit seemed to be the youngest.

"So, now that I know who you all are I would like to know about the victim" Ayaan looked at the body in the office, while Milan was standing right next to him taking notes in his notepad.

"There isn't much to tell really, Mr. Agarwal was always very secretive of his life" said the man with the lowest amount of hair on his head.

"Alright!" Ayaan replied, "tell me all you know about him, any detail can help, why don't you start with his first name"

Ayaan was looking over at Milan's notes while waiting for the answer to the question he just posed. However the answer never came. Realizing that Ayaan looked up to the four men standing with their heads pointed towards their feet.
Ayaan raised an eyebrow, "well? Should I repeat the question?"

The youngest one replied this time, "The thing is Mr. Shahi, we don't actually know his first name"

This was bizarre, Ayaan had no words, and he was stuck on a case where the victim's name was the mystery.

"What?" That were the only words that came out of Ayaan's mouth.

The old man who called himself aadarsh replied "we told you we knew nothing about Mr. Agarwal in particular.

Ayaan didn't speak for some time after that, he let the thought sink in and understand the situation he had at hand. He pulled out the yellow blood stained parchment he had retrieved from the victims pocket and scanned it hoping to find a name that goes before Agarwal. But the parchment was describing an incident about a sultan or something related to it.

He kept it back in his pocket and looked up. The four men were standing in front of him staring at him and waiting for him to act. Their faces were expressionless, it were as if nothing was absurd and everything was... Well normal. It wasn't the case with Ayaan however, and by the looks of Milan's face he wasn't sure about it either.

"Well" Ayaan spoke after a long pause, "You must have company records or account details which would give us Mr. Agarwal's first name right?

"Yeah, but we can't get you that until Monday." Said the near bald old man.

"Monday that's two days later".

"We have weekends off"

"I don't care, there has been a murder, the murder of your boss and I don't care who you have to call, I want all the information I need by the end of this day" .Ayaan said with a little frustration.

Ayaan checked his watch, it read 6:39.
Ayaan was getting late, he had to take Ayman to her school

and as he was making no notable progress here he decided to leave.

He asked Milan to walk with him outside the building.

"Make sure the body reaches city morgue, and ask Anand to give me a post mortem report as fast as he can. Make sure you get as much more information out of these managers before you leave and please don't ask them questions like what car did he drive or what sort of smartphone did he prefer, I want relevant questions" Ayaan instructed Milan

"But I only ask them that because it tells a man character, the car he drives and the phone he uses really tells you the kind of person he is"

"No!" Ayaan retorted, "The character of the person is defined by the people he lives around and judging by the people I just met, Mr. Agarwal doesn't seem to have a very appealing character"

"Alright sir, I will contact you as soon I have something valuable"

Ayaan replied that with a nod. He turned around and looked at the big glass building once more before going to his car and starting the engine.

CHAPTER THREE

The sun had risen completely when Ayaan was driving back home, and the roads were still relatively empty. It was actually nice driving on an empty road, Ayaan wondered, not worrying about idiotic drivers of the city. The transport strike had cleared the road even more, and it felt actually safer without busses and taxis driving around as if they own the road. But the credit has to be given to the late night cricket matches and television serials that prevented people from getting up early in the morning. Ayaan always believed in living his life in a healthy manner. Going to sleep on time and waking up on time. He ate right and exercised from time to time. He didn't have 12 inch muscles or anything but he was fit. However he couldn't get his mind off the case he had at hand and the problem was he couldn't do anything with it because he had absolutely no information other than the cause of death and the appearance of the victim. And in Ayaan's professional experience that wasn't enough to solve a murder case. So Ayaan turned on the radio, in hopes that listening to music would calm him down some more.
But it wasn't music that he got.

"Good morning form RJ Arun, good morning to you early birds out there from the rocking RJ of the rock station 94.5 fm. It's a beautiful morning today and we are going to listen to songs that are going to wake you up and go out. But before that let's talk about the breath taking cricket match we all witnessed last night" and he went on to talk about cricket for a long time, then he continued on world news and that included politics and other stuff that Ayaan didn't care for.

Ayaan reached home without hearing any song and hearing lots about information he didn't require. He parked his car, got out and went to the elevator and pushed the button. But the elevator never came, the elevator was still stuck where it had been when Ayaan left this morning, so Ayaan climbed five flights of stairs to get to his apartment. He opened his apartment door with the keys he had in his pocket.

When he entered his apartment he saw that it was just the way he left it. He walked into the living room, put his briefcase on the sofa and sat down. His maid Salma came from the kitchen with a glass of water. He gulped down the glass in three sips. Ayaan didn't realize how thirsty he was until he finished the glass. His throat had indeed been very dry.

"Should I get another glass" Salma asked politely.

Ayaan shook his head, "is Ayman ready yet she has school in half hour"

"She is in the bathroom, she will be out in a while"

"Go check on her and see if she hasn't fallen asleep in there again"

Salma obeyed and went into his daughters room. Ayaan knew that he would not be able to get Ayman to school on time, but that wasn't his concern at the moment, she was in the fourth grade and even if she missed school today, she wasn't going to miss a lot. Ayaan was very proud of his daughter, she smart and a very fast learner, but the best thing about her was her curiosity, which Ayaan thought she got from him. Ayaan's mind still wondered off to the glass office in the third floor of the Olympus building. He was gathering all the information he already had, which was not a lot, and tried to make sense of all of it. He knew that Mr. Agarwal was murdered by a gunshot to the chest. He knew the shooter wasn't professional because he missed the heart by quite some distance even though he was shooting at close range. He was sure that the shooter was someone Mr. Agarwal knew and he also knew that the yellow parchment he retrieved was meant for him to read and had a strong connection to killer, maybe he was trying to leave a message and communicate with him some way.

He was still thinking about that when his daughter entered the living room. She was wearing a very cute little grey uniform. She was already wearing white socks but didn't have any shoes on yet.

"Good morning sweetheart" Ayaan greeted her daughter and kissed her on her cheek. "Now go and quickly finish your breakfast do we can go to school, come on hurry up".

Silently Ayman Shahi walked to the dinner table and sat down.

Salma came from the kitchen with a bowl of cereal and placed it onto the dinner table. Ayman quietly started eating it.
Ayaan wasn't feeling hungry at the moment, probably because he just came from a crime scene where there was too much blood to digest and now for some time Ayaan didn't feel like digesting anything else. Ayaan saw the newspapers at

27

the side of the sofa. He picked it up and read the date, it was today's newspaper. Ayaan wondered if the news of the murder had reached the media, it wasn't on the city radio probably the newspapers might have snagged up the information somehow. He saw the headlines and was disappointed. The entire front page was about last night's cricket match which was as the newspaper dubbed it "a historic moment for the game". He flipped through the paper and found nothing worth of interest. However he had time to kill until Ayman was ready to go so he read the paper anyway.

He read it for about 10 minutes when Salma called out "Ayman is ready to go".

Ayaan folded the paper neatly and kept it on the sofa and looked at his young daughter. She was standing there quietly and waiting.
Ayaan gestured through the door and she moved out and Ayaan followed.

The elevator was still not functioning so they had to take the stairs. They went to the parking say in the car and Ayaan started the car and took it onto the road. The traffic had increased significantly and it seemed like the road was filled with parents in cars and scooters trying to get their kids to school on time. Ayaan figured that there might actually be a downside to the transport strike. But Ayaan didn't mind dropping off Ayman to school, he loved spending time with her and he was sure she felt the same way. However at the moment she was awfully very quiet, she hadn't spoken a word since morning and Ayaan wondered what was going on with her.

"Hey princess, you alright there?" Ayaan inquired

"Yeah" she replied in a soft but blunt voice.
Ayaan understood.

"Is this about the drama that you mentioned last night, you know I am doing it for your own good, I mean you can do a lot better you deserve better, you understand?"

"Yeah I get it" Ayman replied understandingly

Ayaan looked at her, she was looking plainly out of the window into the road, Ayaan placed his eyes on the road again. Ayaan was sure that she would grow out of it and will understand that what he was doing was best for her. However Ayaan couldn't help recalling what happened last night.

There was a auditioning for a play going on in Ayman's school and Ayman had auditioned after Ayaan advised her for the role of Snow White in their adaptation of the famous story of Snow White and the 7 dwarfs. However Ayman didn't get selected for the role, even though Ayaan knew she was phenomenal in their rehearsals. Last night After Ayaan came home from work he had a bath and both of them sat down for dinner. Ayman then told him that she had gotten a part in the play, Ayaan was very ecstatic and eager to know about the role. It turned she was going to be a tree. Ayaan was disappointed but he did his best to hide it. Ayman was still willing to the role, but Ayaan explained to her about her potential and how much she could achieve and suggested strongly that she should not take the role. Ayman was vividly disappointed and she did not hide it well, Ayaan did just give her a suggestion and the freedom to do as she seemed fit he knew underneath that his daughter would never do anything if he is not 100 percent behind it. Ayaan was always by his peers and family members to reach out and be the best at everything, and he was sure that Ayman was the best in her class and he didn't want her to settle. Ayaan had completely forgotten about last night until just now, so much had happened since then, he had much important things to concentrate on. But now he felt it was the right time to talk about the elephant in the room and so he did.

They rode at 20kmph in busy traffic, it was tedious and tiresome. Somewhere close to reaching the school, Ayman asked "dad do I need to start wearing a veil"

Ayaan turned his head towards her and she was staring right into his face. She looked as cute as she had ever been. Ayaan looked at her eyes trying to find the best answer to her question. Ayman had his dad's eyes, one Ayaan had stared into lots of times when he was young.

Ayaan remembered one conversation with his dad which was based on something Ayaan had very curiously asked. He might have been the same age as Ayman was right now maybe even younger. He had stared into his dad's eyes the same as the ones he was staring in right now and asked "dad, the kids in the society say that I need to go to the mosque 5 times a day or God will burn me alive after I am dead."

His dad just gave him the biggest smile he had seen and said "what do you think?"

"I don't know, I mean they say God loves you 100 times more than your mom, and if I don't visit mummy five times a day she will not burn me, so if God loves me so much why would he do something like that?"

30

Ayaan remembered his dad laughing loudly "then do what you believe to be true, listen to me Ayaan, in the future there will be a lot of people telling you lots of things to do, all you need to do is stay true to yourself and you are staying true to God"

Ayaan remembered this conversation with his dad more vividly than any other he had, because this conversation shaped his whole life up till now. To this day he had always stayed true to himself and when it came to religion he had found his own way to be grateful to the almighty.

"Why you ask" Ayaan inquired

"Because some of the senior girls in school wear it and they say to me that I should start wearing it too. They say it's customary to wear won if you don't want to die a horrible death and have a miserable afterlife"

She said it in such a polite manner that Ayaan didn't even realize she used the word death and miserable afterlife in there.

However Ayaan smiled and said "Do what you think is right sweet heart, you can wear it and if you don't feel like it you can take it off, it completely your choice. Just remember that there are only two kinds of people in the world, ones who are true to themselves and live their lives the way they like and do things that they seem fit and others are ones who live their lives based on what other people would see them as, you have to decide which one you want to be"

Ayman didn't reply, but Ayaan sensed that she understood what he was trying to say.

It took them approximately 5 minutes to reach Ayman's school. It was a pale yellow building which seemed to be a 100 years old, and it was surrounded by walls and gates. The scene at the entrance of the school was chaotic, parents rushing their children inside, everyone seemed to be late Ayaan thought. Ayaan stooped the car in front of the gate and Ayman got out, as she took two steps out of the car Ayaan said, "I will pick you up at noon and remember what I said alright? Go and enjoy yourself"

Ayman nodded and walked into the gate with her bag on her shoulders. Ayaan waited for some time to see his daughter go safely inside and then he drove away.

CHAPTER FOUR

He went home the same way he had come to the school, and he unfortunately had to face the same old traffic while coming back. It seemed like just like him all the other parents who had dropped their kids to school were now going back to drop in bed. Ayaan was an early bird, but he had to wake up very early in the morning today so he was getting sleepy as well. He was yawning at an astounding 3 yawns per minute and his yawns were long and deep. His eyes felt tired and he was feeling really drowsy. Slowly and steadily at 20kmph he made his back to the building.

He didn't even bother calling the elevator because he had lost all hope in it. He just climbed up 5 flights of stairs and rang the doorbell. He had the keys but he was feeling too lazy to reach them out of his pockets and open the door. Just some seconds later Salma opened the door and Ayaan walked in, greeted her and directly went into his room.

He untucked his shirt, took out the belt he was wearing on his pants and put it aside. He had totally forgotten about his gun and he had carried it to school where little children were all around, it was good that he had not gotten out of his car. Ayaan felt stupid to forget about his gun, but he was too sleepy to think about it a lot, so he just put the gun on his dresser next to his bed and dropped in his bed.

Time passed and all Ayaan did was roll over in bed trying to sleep. He felt drowsy, his eyes were heavy but he couldn't fall asleep. This wasn't the first time this had happened, he was an insomniac when he was a kid. He had trouble sleeping, probably because he thought a lot about all the stuff going on with him and didn't free his mind enough to fall asleep. But Ayaan was much older now, he was 38 years old and he knew he had to free his mind to fall asleep, yet no matter how much he tried he was unsuccessful.

Ayaan finally opened his eyes and saw the watch next to his bed, it read 9:29. He had been trying to sleep for over an hour and still he felt tired and exhausted. He saw his gun placed on the dresser next to the watch.

 His brain took him directly to three years in the past, when he was young, not very young but definitely younger than he is today. When he thought of the Ayaan of the past he realized how much of a fool he was back then, how many things he still had to learn and how much pain he still had to bear.

 Pain, that burning pain, Ayaan's hand went to his left shoulder where the scar still remained, faint but still evident. It was the result of a kidnapping case gone wrong, really wrong. It was the Chopra's 8 year-old-boy who had been abducted and Ayaan courageously no doubt but also stupidly took situation in his own hands. The gang was known for its sincere threats and Ayaan was assigned to the case to overlook the money transaction. Ayaan tried to be a hero for the first time in his life and it taught him never to try and be one again.

One of the gang members fired a bullet aiming for his heart he was sure, but fortunately missed. He had gathered enough strength to run for his life and ended up beaten and bloodied at the side of the road. It had been so long but Ayaan still could feel what he had felt that night, it felt like someone was sucking all the blood out of his body and he didn't know he was not did he have the strength to stop him. His mind had stopped and his heart was slowing down, he had enough time to have his whole life flash in front of his eyes. That night he saw everything and everyone, from his father to his daughter, he experienced sorrow and joy at the same time. At that time he knew he had had a good life but he also knew he wanted to live a little more. So with all the little strength he could muster he called the only person he knew would come to his aid at once, his newly employed, passionate and zeal assistant Chetak.

Chetak Milan's small round face came into Ayaan's mind and he decided to call him.

Ayaan couldn't fall asleep so he decided to focus on the case at hand. Ayaan was a person who always wanted to be up to date with what was happening around him and this was also the scenario with his cases. He always wanted to know what was happening with the case at hand even when he wasn't present.

That was one of the reasons why he admired Milan's work so much, because doesn't matter what he was always up to date with the case.

Ayaan had a nice and long 15 minute chat with Milan over the phone. In their conversation Ayaan asked everything that had happened after he had left the office of Mr. Agarwal. Milan informed him that the four people whose name Ayaan didn't care to remember had left shortly after he did. The paramedics had arrived also and the dead body was taken to the city morgue for examination. Dr. Anand was assigned to examine the body and he informed Milan that it would take him a couple of days at least to give them a thorough report of the body. He asked Milan to make sure that by the end of the day he at least finds out the name of the victim and any more information that could aide them in solving this case, Milan agreed and he hung up the phone.

Ayaan considered the case for moment, and no matter how much he tried he couldn't shake off the feeling that something was definitely not in place with this case. Everything from the way he got this case to the person he got it from to the cause of death to the information about the victim, everything had a piece missing. It was like he was trying to find a missing piece of a puzzle but as soon as he found it he realized that he didn't have the puzzle in the first place.

Ayaan thought he was overthinking this too much, he always did that. He discovered that maybe after he had had enough information and a right mind he would turn this feeling around and find a way to eventually solve this case. He was a private investigator after all, he made a living by solving cases. Probably the only one in the city able to do so.

He laid down in his bed thinking, when he realized he had something in his pocket. He was still very sleepy, but he took out whatever was in there and took it out to have a look. He had completely forgotten about this, the yellow parchment stained with Mr. Agarwal's blood was still with him enclosed within a plastic bag, marked evidence.

For whatever reason Ayaan knew that this letter was the key to solving this case, the problem was he had a key but no lock to unlock. He read what he could through the plastic bag. He wasn't wearing his gloves and he didn't wanted to tamper with what he thought was a very essential evidence relating with the case. He read the title again, "the pious drunkard and fornicator". He had this feeling that he had read this before, but he couldn't remember what it was about. He had a faded memory of reading something like this when he was young, however he couldn't recall anything right now. He had to get this parchment to the city morgue to check for any fingerprints, to Dr. Anand. Dr. Anand was a very talented, genuine and professional doctor. Ayaan knew him ever since he started as a private investigator and he respected him a lot. Dr. Anand's reports were rock solid, not a thing missing, everything was mentioned in that report. From the cause of death to the last time the subject had any food. His reports were thorough and precise, probably why he took so long to have them ready, but Ayaan didn't mind, he wanted quality and that's what he would be getting. Ayaan wanted to read more of what was written in the parchment he had in his hand, but again he couldn't get past reading the main title. His eyes were getting heavy again and he was feeling very tired all of a sudden. He decided to try and fall asleep once more, with luck he might be able to accomplish that this time. He checked the watch on his dressing table, it read 11:03, he had roughly just above an hour to sleep. After that he had to run to his daughter's school and pick her up again. The idea of that made Ayaan feeling exhausted, nevertheless if Ayaan fell asleep this very minute he would be fresh enough to do the task.

Ayaan did not fall asleep that very minute, he didn't fall asleep that very hour also, he had set his alarm for 12:20, and the last time Ayaan had dared check his clock, it was 12 already. Ayaan gave up on the idea of falling asleep, because up till now he knew he was not going to succeed at it. He felt fatigued and exhausted so he decided to just lay in bed with his eyes closed and rest and Ayaan dreamed.

CHAPTER FIVE

Ayaan was standing in a big room, it was dark but Ayaan could still make out where he was. He had a bag in his hand it was heavy so Ayaan put it aside. He knew where he was so Ayaan went to the far end of the room and found the switch board to turn on the lights. The room was well lit now and Ayaan saw what he already knew. He saw the punching bag in one corner and weights and Dumbbells on the other side, he was without a doubt in his gymnasium. He came here thrice a week to box and workout.

He loved boxing form a very young age, he also loved looking after himself and boxing was a great workout for him. He knew where he was but had no idea why he was here, the gym was completely empty, and no one was in sight not even his trainer. He saw to doors in the room at opposite sides of the room. He knew where those doors led to. One would lead him out and the other to the boxing ring and shower room. He knew the boxing ring very well, he had participated in many tiny competitions, which were organized just for fun, for guys like him to compete and enjoy boxing as a sport. He decided to leave, he clearly wasn't here at the right time, and he knew that. He went to the door and tried to unlock only to fail. He tried harder but the door wouldn't budge, it was locked shut. It seemed like he had no choice but to stay put. So he decided to make the most of the situation he had at hand. He put on his gear from the bag he had put aside and was ready to workout. He went to the second door and tried to unlock that. And surprisingly it worked the door flew open and Ayaan went through. He took a long shower and came back into the empty room to do some weights.

He discovered that the room wasn't empty anymore, he saw a man sitting on a chair next to the punching bag. Ayaan stopped and saw his long deceased father in front of him. He saw him and got up from his chair smiling. He said something, but Ayaan didn't hear it. Ayaan saw his mouth open and close but couldn't make out what he was trying to say. He saw him smiling again, grinning through his long and thick beard. Ayaan knew his father was telling him something important and Ayaan had to know what it was. Ayaan moved closer to him in the attempt to understand what he was saying. His father opened his mouth but all Ayaan could here was a loud ringing noise. It was so loud that Ayaan had to cover his ears and he saw his father smiling still and it seemed that the loud noise didn't affect him. He shut his eyes and opened it to wake up in his room to an alarm clock ringing.

He checked the time on the clock, it was 12 20 already. He had just got 20 minutes of sleep and was urging for more, but he knew he couldn't. His daughter would be out of school in some time and he had to bring her back home. The only problem was that he was way to sleepy to do anything at the moment.

After much struggle he picked himself out of bed and went to the bathroom to freshen up. He splashed water on his face a couple of times to wake himself up. He then got out of his room, he went to the dining table pulled up a chair and sat down comfortably. Salma was also in the room dusting the curtains and doing daily cleaning work. Ayaan preferred it this way, he always wanted his house to look welcoming and most of all habitable. He didn't like mess although he created a lot himself, but he always cleaned it up afterwards.

Salma stopped what she was doing and turned to Ayaan after she realized he was in the room.

"Do you need anything Ayaan sahib" she asked politely

Ayaan realized that he did, he knew he was too exhausted to drive like this so go needed something that would really wake him up

"Make me some coffee quickly please"

"Yes sure, should I make it hot or cold"

"Cold"

Salma didn't ask any further questions but went straight through to the kitchen.

Ayaan was sitting at the dining table waiting for his coffee, he had nothing to do but wait. He turned his head towards the dining table and he saw a piece of paper that he had forgotten about. He reached across the table to grab it. He turned it upside and had a glance at it. The argument with his daughter came into his mind once more about her being in a play, but it didn't stay there long because now he knew that Ayman wasn't upset about it anymore. Of course he wasn't sure about that, he knew his daughter very well and she was a little upset, but Ayaan knew that she would get over it soon. The paper read,

"Dear parent/guardian, this letter is to inform you that Jesus and Mary middle school is organizing its annual drama day. If your child is willing to take part in this event we would like your acknowledgement. Thanking you."

And at the end was blank space with the word "signature" typed on it. Ayaan had decided to let it stay blank, he was still rock solid on his decision and put the paper aside. He should have thrown, Ayaan was willing too also, but he was too lazy to do it right now, maybe later.

Ayaan had to wait a couple of more minutes for his coffee, but he drank it as quickly as Salma brought it to him. The coffee was warm and a little strong for Ayaan's taste but he didn't mind, he had to get going.

The next hour was a total mood killer for Ayaan. The traffic was worse than ever, even without busses and taxis. Ayaan picked up Ayman from her school and brought her back home. She quickly dropped her bag into her room and came into the living room, turned on the TV and forgot everything around her. She was addicted to this teenage pop star TV show, which was funny and kind of nice. Ayaan didn't mind it, at least his daughter was not watching some lame soap that was running before she was even born. Ayman was very smart for her age kind of like Ayaan was when he was this little. Ayaan was sitting on the sofa watching what his daughter was watching, this happened a lot, and Ayaan didn't watch a lot of TV so anything Ayman watched he watched it with her.

Ayaan was totally engrossed in the TV, so much that when his mobile rang he hardly seemed to hear it. It was the vibration that gave him the idea that his phone was actually ringing. Even though his eyes were fixed on the television screen his mind was always on the office doors of Mr. Agarwal. He was trying to decipher the case code by code in his mind.

He checked the caller id on his ringing phone and it read, commissioner Vishnu. Ayaan knew what this phone call was about even before he answered it. It was "what have you done till now" phone call and he got this phone call every time commissioner Vishnu had assigned him to a case. This phone call was always about him trying to portray his superiority over the fact that he is responsible for giving Ayaan the case and he should be given that credit, even though he didn't deserve it. He never wished Ayaan good luck or even appreciate his effort in trying to solve the case, which Ayaan found extremely annoying. Ayaan had dreaded this call ever since Milan told him that the commissioner had insisted on Ayaan getting this case.

Nevertheless Ayaan couldn't ignore this call, so he picked it up.

"Hello" Ayaan said

"Ayaan my boy! How are you?" Said an excited thick voice from the other end. Ayaan didn't get why he would call him a boy, he was less than 10 years older than Ayaan. It had always been this way and Ayaan couldn't really understand the reason.

"Commissioner Vishnu sir, I am great how are you sir"

"Enough with the small talk Ayaan, let's talk business" the commissioner snapped, even though began the conversation and Ayaan was just being polite.

"Well I would really like to thank you for the case" said Ayaan not meaning it at all.

"Well I guess you should be, I am counting on you kid, do a good job and solve it as fast as you can."

"Yes sir"

"I want you to know that ever since I got this case you were my first pick and I don't want to be disappointed."

Ayaan knew that all the commissioner said right now was garbage, he knew that commissioner Vishnu would never pick him first, unless it was too dangerous or too insignificant to him. He didn't quite know why he picked him for this case, but Ayaan knew that the commissioner had an agenda of his own.

The commissioner went on to brag about his previous cases that he had assigned Ayaan to and to portray his superiority over Ayaan as the commissioner of the city. The call lasted for 21 minutes and after it ended Ayaan knew that he had wasted a lot of precious time that he would never get back.

CHAPTER SIX

More than a day and a half had passed since that phone call and the weekend was already over. It was Monday morning and everything was the way it should be. The transport strike had ended so Ayaan didn't have to go and drop Ayman to school, which meant he could sleep a little longer. However that didn't make a lot of difference because Ayaan was having trouble sleeping, he seemed to have developed insomnia. He didn't know exactly why he might have developed it, but it was certainly connected to the case he was working on.

Not a lot had happened in the day and a half that had passed. Ayaan had asked Milan to contact the managers of the firm and get solid information about Mr. Agarwal, but according to Milan the managers were very ignorant to his phone calls. He hadn't been able to get in touch with them either, it really made Ayaan furious, he didn't expect such them to be so unprofessional. Mr. Agarwal was their boss and even though he might have not been a great boss, which Ayaan seemed was a fair and justified assumption, he was dead and that fact needed to be respected. Nevertheless Ayaan had decided to go to the office again personally and confront the managers and also talk to the staff and get as much information out as possible. He wanted to close this case as quickly as possible and he was confident that he would. It was 11 am in the morning, Ayman was at school, Ayaan was out of bed in the living room in the sofa reading the morning news paper. He had already had his bath and was dressed too. He had 2 cups of coffee and was pumped up with caffeine. He felt pretty good about today, he knew that he would crack this case once and for all.

He had asked Chetak to be at the Olympus building at precisely 12 and that's when Ayaan intended to reach. Ayaan knew offices in the city and he knew the employees who worked in offices, when the boss asked everyone to report at 9, it meant he doesn't expect you to show up till 10. That's how it worked and Ayaan didn't believe in following that norm. He always wanted to be punctual, on time, before time if necessary but never late. He lived by that rule and he taught his daughter to do exactly that too. Ayaan was reading the newspaper, well not exactly reading the news scanning it.

He was trying to find whether there was an article about the case in the paper. He had checked it yesterday also but there wasn't any. Ayaan didn't quite understand why there wasn't any word going around town about a murder in a big corporation. This was a pretty safe city and cases like this didn't stay hidden for too long, even if people tried. Police officials and detectives always liked to keep the cases away from the media, but Ayaan thought it didn't matter, the more people know about the case the more alert they will be if anything happens. So Ayaan never prevented or try to stop the media from getting the news, heck, Ayaan even gave interviews regarding cases. However there was no mention about the current case whatsoever, Ayaan was certainly puzzled but he figured that once he gets ahead in the case there will something substantial to talk about it and then probably the media will cover it. It was hard to stay optimistic about this but somehow Ayaan managed.

However, it was time now for Ayaan to go to work. He knew he had to leave a little early as today was a working day and he was bound to run into some traffic. He wished he didn't but he couldn't help but be a little pessimistic. He followed the same routine he had followed ever since he had become a private investigator, he got his briefcase, got his business card, put got his car keys and of course his latest addition to his list of essentials, a 9mm handgun. He got all of those things and headed down. Fortunately he didn't have to climb down five flights of stairs, the elevator was functioning. So all he had to do was press a button and he was on the ground floor. He walked to his car in his parking, unlocked it and drove it out. The traffic wasn't that bad according to Ayaan. The last time he went to the Olympus building it took him ten minutes, not it was more like a half hour, but Ayaan knew this city very well, he had lived his entire life here for all he cared it could have been worse. Ayaan reached Olympus building but couldn't find Milan anywhere, he checked his watch and confirmed what he already was skeptical about, he was before time, and outstanding 20 minutes before time. He would have to wait for Milan. Ayaan didn't mind it though, he liked being early for things, it helped him to get mentally prepared for the things he might encounter and give him some time to brainstorm.

Ayaan took the time to imagine every possible event that might transpire when he walked through the glass sliding doors with the earth picture embossed on it and go to the elevator and press for the third floor. Some of His imaginations got bizarre too, he even imagined what it would be like to walk in and discover that this case was all a sham and witness Mr. Agarwal fit and healthy standing in front of him. Of course it was insane of him to imagine that but Ayaan couldn't help but shake of the weird feeling he had about the case. He getting the case without even asking for one from perhaps the most selfish guy he knew, it was just a recipe for disaster.

It had already been 12 minutes and Ayaan was still waiting, and Ayaan was already mentally prepared for scenarios which involved hand to hand combat and also scenarios which made Ayaan feel safer that he had not forgotten his gun.

Ayaan then saw someone driving a two wheeler into the lane. He knew it was Milan but couldn't make sure what he was driving. He pulled up close and it was ironic Ayaan felt. Chetak driving a Chetak, Ayaan didn't laugh of course he would have offended Milan but he couldn't help but feel a little amused.

Ayaan waited while Milan parked the scooter and got his essentials with him to join Ayaan. They didn't have anything to discuss this time, frankly because they had made any progress in the case whatsoever. In any other criminal case which Ayaan was in charge of, Ayaan would have already solved half of it if not more. Ayaan believed in dedication, that's what his father had taught him, so whenever he got a case like the one he currently was working on he thought about it all day and all night, and with strength and sagacity, hope and stern pertinacity, and of course a little bit of luck he always did it faster and better than anyone else would, probably why he was the best in the city. He knew he was but he always liked to work as if it was the first case he was working on. But unfortunately with this case he was stuck awfully and the lack of information he had was the reason of this delay. Nevertheless Ayaan was here now and he was ready to take this case on, and get all that he should have gotten way before. He entered through the glass doors with the picture of the earth and the quote "You are entering a different world" which was more ironic than ever now. He entered the lobby and was about to go for the elevator which would take him to the third floor and to the murder scene of the most absurd criminal case he had ever encountered, when a voice called out "Yes! May I help you"?

Ayaan turned to his right and found a table which he had completely failed to notice, probably because there was no one there at that point, but now there was a woman dressed in purple and blue with black glasses sitting on that very table.

Ayaan and Milan both went towards the lady and Milan spoke
    "umm, we are here for the Mr. Agarwal ca.."

    "Wait" she cut Milan off, "let me see if he has come in today"
As she picked up the phone in her table to dial, Ayaan shared a very confusing look with Milan and Milan's hand gesture suggested the same think Ayaan was thinking at that very moment, what the hell is going on?

The lady kept the phone down and turned her attention towards the two men, "well he is not in today, he isn't answering his cell phone so probably on a foreign trip, and if that's the case you would have to come back in a week"
Ayaan was confused, astounded, perplexed and baffled all the same time, he had imagined so many possible scenarios waiting outside he never in his wildest dreams thought this could be one. The lady had no idea about Mr. Agarwal's murder

    "How long have you been working here" Ayaan inquired out of sheer curiosity, hoping the answer to be "this morning"

"7 years now" she answered almost ostentatiously
It made no sense whatsoever

"And you have no idea what has happened with Mr.
Agarwal?"

"Well you know he takes a lot of trips out of country so I
just wondered he might be on one right now, I can give him
your message if you like"

Ayaan scratched his head and looked at Milan for answers
and found nothing, he was as puzzled as Ayaan himself was.
Ayaan didn't know what exactly he could do so he decided to
play along

"Yes miss, I would like to leave a message, actually it's not
a message just a bunch of questions I have for Mr. Agarwal"

She took a note pad and was ready to write
"Does it hurt to take a bullet to the chest and bleed to
death, what is it like after death and how is heaven like and
unless you didn't make it there, how is hell like?"

"Are you like a crazy person" the lady said scrutinizing
Ayaan intently, "because Mr. Agarwal has a lot of people
who are like crazy, he himself is a little like that. Did you
know he shaved his head because he wanted to hide the fact
that he was losing hair?"

Ayaan didn't know how to respond to that, he was a crazy
person? Everything around him was crazy and he thought he
was the only one around here to be sane. Ayaan was getting
frustrated and he didn't want that, so he took a deep breath,

51

looked at the lady on the front desk with as much politeness he could muster "alright, it's fine that Mr. Agarwal isn't here, can I talk to the manager umm Mr. Gandhi?" His was the only name Ayaan could remember from the four people he met day before yesterday. Ayaan hoped that the lady would at least know about this person.

"Aha! Mr. Praveen Gandhi, yes he is the advertising and marketing manager, he isn't here today though, he is gone for a very important business trip. He will be back in two days, you can come back then, and he usually comes in at around 10 and leaves in the evening. You can meet him anytime in between"

That was a lot of information about a very unimportant person, Ayaan thought. Ayaan was however relived that the lady knew something even though it wasn't about the owner of the company, who should be the person everyone should have the most information about. Ayaan thanked her and asked her to visit the office anyway, she didn't refute much and let Ayaan have his way. Ayaan and Milan went to the elevator and pressed for the third floor. The button glowed and the doors of the elevator shut.

"What do we do now sir, this case seems like a lost cause" Milan spoke
Ayaan was battling with the same idea himself, he was trying to reassure himself that there was still more to the case than what meets the eye. But what if there wasn't, what if this is as far as the case goes, a dead man without a first name, dead with a bullet wound in an office that he built where no one really knows who he is. As a private investigator, Ayaan always knew he might come across a case which can't be solved, an unusual case with an incomplete story. However Ayaan was still hopeful that he was going to solve this case

and he might find some leads today.

"We do what we do best, we investigate"

The elevator doors opened into the third floor. Straight away Ayaan could here loud noises of people talking on phones and to each other about business and more. He walked into the passageway which was filled with cubicles on either side and in the far end of the he could see that glass office where he saw the victim. The inside of the office wasn't visible, the curtains were down and therefore was obstructing the view.

"Hand me over the balance sheet for the last quarter" said one man to another

"We have not yet received the goods sir" said another man talking on the phone

"I can't offer you a lower price, you will have to talk to my manager" said one other man on the phone as well. The room was chaotic and Ayaan was standing in the midst of it.

He tried asking several busy employees who were dressed in white shirts and were wearing different colored ties about Mr. Agarwal, all anyone did was point to the office where he was murdered. Whether they were telling Ayaan to go meet Mr. Agarwal in the office or towards the murder scene itself Ayaan couldn't tell. But after nearly asking five people the same question and getting no absolute answer, he was done with it. Ayaan didn't get enraged very often, but today there was no avoiding it. He could feel the frustration and his hands clenched to become a fist. He asked Milan to quite everyone down with controlled anger and headed into Mr. Agarwal's office.

He was half expecting to still see the blood stains in the chair and the room floor, but fortunately they were wiped clean, at least someone knew something had happened, it's not every day that you find a pool of blood in an office. He turned his head around to see if anything had been altered since he last visited this place, but things seemed to be intact or as long as Ayaan could remember. He saw the curtain drawn in the office which completely obscured the view to what was going on the outside, he decided to change that. He opened the curtains which were heavy and colored with red, kind of like Mr. Agarwal's blood.

He walked out of the office to find a silent hall and over 50 clueless heads all pointed towards him. He didn't know how Milan accomplished this but he couldn't help but feel impressed, clearly whatever Milan might have said Ayaan couldn't hear it in the office.

Ayaan began "since no one of you knows who I am or why the hell I am stopping you from doing your job let me introduce myself. I am private investigator Ayaan Shahi this is my associate Milan and we are here regarding the murder of your boss and this company's owner Mr. Agarwal." Some chatters followed the room, some were aghast by discovering this for the first time, this 'some' were to Ayaan's despair most.

However Ayaan did notice some employees not displaying any strong reaction whatsoever, either they already knew about this or they were hiding something that Ayaan ought to know.

"Clearly most of you are hearing about this for the first time which is sad" Ayaan continued in a stern voice, "I am here to request for your assistance to finish my job, I want information that is all I ask about the victim your boss. Any information will do, and I would like to start with you providing me with his first name"

Ayaan paused for answers, his previous encounters had made him think that he would get what he least preferred, a stun silence, but the case was otherwise. He got a response alright, he got several responses, one from everyone in the room, and some even gave two of them.

"Mahesh" said one

"No no, it's Malav

"It's Sanjiv"

" Rahul"

"Uday"

" Upesh "

" Ajit "

"Kabir"

"Harman"

"Jaru "

"Bhuvan"

And tons more. Ayaan even believed to hear someone say "I heard someone say Ayaan once". But no answer was certain and I Ayaan gave up. He asked unwillingly for everyone to return back to their respective works, however people didn't stop guessing names

"I know it's starts with a k"

"Probably Jeet"

"Umm I think Dev"

Ayaan was still pondering over his next step towards solving the case and by the looks of it Milan was doing the same thing. Ayaan knew what Milan was capable of, he was a smart kid, who when Ayaan missed something important or even something unimportant he would be the one to point him out, more than that he was a really good friend, one of the closest Ayaan had had in years. So if Ayaan was stuck and Milan didn't know a way out either they were in for a big problem.

They were still in the middle of brainstorming through this debacle, when a they heard a voice, it was low and was just more than a whisper, Ayaan looked up to see a man, who was just like the others, dressed the same way, looked kind of similar too, and listened

"I know something you might want to hear"

Ayaan exchanged intent looks with Milan, was this is it, was this the turning of this case, will he get the information he needs from this anonymous person. Ayaan tried not to get his hopes up, he didn't want to seem too eager.

"What is it" Ayaan asked humbly

"Not here, follow me"

The strange man walked past the office took a right and went into a room, which wasn't actually a room but a passageway that led to more offices. Ayaan followed him and so did Milan. There was a water dispenser and a table on which a coffee maker was placed, used and unused coffee mugs were kept on the table. Ayaan waited for the man to talk, but Ayaan was curious so he started

"Who are you and what do you know?"

"Who am I is not important but what I know is" he said very timidly

"I may not know a lot but I know something that might help you solve the case"

"What?" Milan jumped in

"I know who the murderer is"

Ayaan couldn't help but feel appalled, this guy with no certain credibility knows who the murderer of Mr. Agarwal is? That seemed strange and suspicious too. By the looks of it, the man didn't look anything special, he had one of the faces that you might forget, not very special and part of the crowd. He wasn't dressed special too, he wore an un-ironed white shirt and a grey tie over it. But this person was the biggest lead Ayaan had gotten in this case, he wasn't going to squander that over a technicality. He might be correct for all he knew, so with suspicion, impatience, desperation and a little frustration Ayaan asked "who?"

"I am not sure if you are aware of the fact but there is a place called the coined cathedral"
Ayaan's mind froze he did not like where this was headed

"Well it's a gambling den and people from all around the city who are fond or addicted to gambling are found there, it is probably the biggest and the only spot to that in the city. Mr. Agarwal was frequent there as well, he suffered from a gambling addiction I hear and was lately in a huge debt with the person who runs that place. The owner of the place is a dangerous man and one who doesn't take kindly to people who don't pay his debts. He is the one you should talk to, he is the one behind all of this, but be careful he is a very powerful man, I don't know his name but he is mostly goes by"

And then Ayaan heard the strange man say the absolute last name he wanted to hear

"The father"

CHAPTER SEVEN

Ayaan drove home thinking about the case. If Mr. Agarwal was involved with these sorts of people then he must be in huge trouble. Ayaan knew what kinds of things went down on the so call 'coined cathedral' and if Mr. Agarwal was somehow a part of it, he was meddling with some very powerful people, deadly even. Ayaan knew this very well, hell everyone in the city who had lived here long enough knew how dangerous it could be.

Ayaan had discussed this with Milan after their brief conversation with the stranger from the office, they had decided upon meeting tonight at 10 to visit and confront 'the father'.

But Ayaan didn't want to think about that right now, he will deal with it later.

Ayaan turned on the radio and decided to listen to some music, he didn't get to listen to it a lot as radios were anyways more of talking and less of music. However baring to all the gibberish talks and the ridiculous advertisements he made it to his apartment. He placed his car in the parking and got out, he was about to go to the elevator and into the his home and relax for a while, clear his head so he could think better, but he was stopped in his tracks. He heard someone call out his name

"Ayaan! Ayaan wait up!"

He knew this voice and he turned to confirm it.

And there she was standing in a purple dress with a black purse in her right hand, big sunglasses which came till her nose and heels that made her look taller than Ayaan.

Barsha Bakshi lived two floors below Ayaan and she was a good friend. Barsha was single divorced mother who was around in in her mid-30s not a lot younger than Ayaan himself, but she dressed like she was twenty, talked like she was eighteen and had a daughter who was ten. That was one of the main reason Ayaan was friend with Barsha, her only daughter Preeti was great friends with Ayman, they went to the same school, travelled together and were in the same grade as well. It was safe to say that they were best friends. And Ayaan didn't mind Ayman hanging out with Preeti, she was sweet and well behaved. In addition Barsha was always ready to baby sit for Ayman and let her stay at her place when Ayaan had a case and had to stay away from home for long. Ayaan didn't mind her company too, she was smart and kind. The only flaw she had, in Ayaan's opinion was that she bragged a lot. She was a kind of person who needed to flaunt everything she had, and that was reflected in her dressing choice as well. But Ayaan had learned to look past that. However at first Ayaan admitted to really dislike her as person, not because she did anything, just because everyone else in the building disliked her as well. A divorcee who still looked really pretty kind of made everyone else uncomfortable. She was called many names when she initially moved in 6 years ago, man seeker, slut, bitch and many other derogatory terms that Ayaan didn't want to think about. It was after he got to know her on a personal level that he realized how wrong he had been all along about this women.

"Oh man. Walking in these heels is a pain in the ass" she complained

"Well I wouldn't know about it a lot"

"You are lucky, driving in these things is hard work, and this damn transport strike led me to drive Preeti all the way to school and back, my feet were so sore, I had to get a full body massage on Sunday just to ease the pain. The one ride cost 3500 bucks"

Ayaan smiled he knew this was coming "well I think you will have to go tomorrow as well, because it looks like the elevator is stuck again"

" oh shit, it looks like those old hags on the 9th floor can't seem to find a way to shut the elevator door properly, well nothing to be done, walk up with me will you"
Ayaan agreed and they both started walking up the stairs

"Did you know" she continued "Preeti auditioned and got selected as a lead in the play they are doing at school"
Ayaan did know but didn't want to mention it

"Is Ayman participating?" She questioned

"No no she isn't" Ayaan replied

"Oh that's fine, I mean Preeti is a great actor I know she will make me proud"
Ayaan nodded in agreement.

They were nearing to the third floor, where Barsha lived.
"So what's new Ayaan, any new case you have been working on?"

That was the last thing Ayaan wanted to talk about right now, but he knew he would have to answer it anyway.

"Umm yes actually" and then Ayaan went on to explain everything about the case so far

"Huh, this sounds boring, I would have given up already"
And with that statement she went into her apartment.

Ayaan didn't think about that too much and he climbed up two stories and went into his apartment. The living room was empty, the curtains were drawn and the windows were open. Sharp Sun Rays were filling the room and it was hot. The glare was blinding so Ayaan shut the windows and drew the curtains. Now it was more peaceful and cosier. Ayaan hadn't had lunch and it was already 2, and his stomach was rumbling. He would have called out for Salma and ask her to serve lunch for him, but Ayaan knew that she might be sleeping at this hour, it was her afternoon nap time. And she did so much for Ayaan and compared to that Ayaan paid her peanuts. She was the one who looked after the house day in and day out, whether Ayaan was present or absent she made sure the apartment was habitable. Ayaan hired her after his wife passed away, and she has taken care of this house ever since. She was loyal and trustworthy, two attributes that Ayaan respected dearly, and Ayaan knew how difficult it was to find such qualities in people these days, and that's why they were so special to Ayaan, that's why she was special to Ayaan.

However Ayaan was still hungry and kind of exhausted, but he couldn't sleep on an empty stomach, he needed something, he saw the fruit basket kept on the dining table and in it he saw 2 bananas and an orange. Ayaan ate all of it. He also saw the paper that asked for the parents' consent regarding the school play in Ayman's school. Ayaan didn't know why it was still here, he was not going to sign it, might as well throw it in the trash. But he would have to do it some other time or ask Salma to do it.

Ayaan needed to clear his mind right now, freedom from thoughts is what he required. He hadn't had a full night's sleep in two days, he was building insomnia, every night sleep eluded him more and more. Ayaan didn't like to oversleep but he didn't like sleep which was less as well. He always aimed to sleep the right amount and wake up fresh and fine. That wasn't going on for him for the past couple of days, and He would have done anything to change it.

The clock struck 9 in no time, Ayaan had dinner with Ayman and she was getting ready for bed. It had been a long day for Ayaan and it was about to get longer. Ayaan was going to go to the coined cathedral to investigate and he knew how bad it could get. He had had four cups of coffee already and was wide awake. He needed to be vigilante and alert, one misstep and things could go really wrong. However something did happen that was kind of positive this evening. Ayaan had received another case already. He didn't really want to call it a case, because it was merely anything more than stalking, but it was a case nonetheless. The client was a family he had already worked with in the past, the Guptas. He was assigned to their case some 7 years ago, he couldn't even remember what that case exactly was, he had done so many other cases for them after that. Payal Gupta was his main client after the first case, she was very impressed by his determination and approach towards his work so she had offered him lots of other cases. All the cases basically revolved around the same idea, of her believing that her husband was cheating on her with another woman. She had confessed to Ayaan on numerous occasions that she loved her husband, but how loving someone and not trusting them works Ayaan couldn't comprehend. These were really lame and tedious cases in Ayaans opinion and something Ayaan would never accept from antithetical client. However Mrs. Gupta really made him an offer he couldn't refuse. Now Ayaan wasn't anything about the money, he would do cases for free if they were interesting and challenging enough and he had done them in the past, but he still had to pay the bills. And unless the electric company, the water company, the gas company and the bank all were in need of hiring a private investigator for a case every month, it wouldn't work. So Ayaan took these cases, which in the end proved nothing except that Payal Gupta was a jealous housewife with no real work to do than doubt her husband for a living. Plus he knew Prakash Gupta on a personal level and he seemed like a genuine guy to him. Nevertheless Ayaan thought of assigning this case to Milan like he had done before, there was no need for him to indulge in it. Milan could learn from this type of case and it could help him late on and Ayaan could focus his attention on the Agarwal case.

Ayaan checked his watch, it was 9 30, and he was late. He needed to get to the place by 10 and this place wasn't close by. He quickly got all the things he required especially his gun, he would require that the most. He couldn't risk forgetting that tonight. He put his gun in the holster and tucked it in his belt. He went downstairs got into his car and drove out.

On the way to coined cathedral Ayaan passed his gymnasium, he looked up to it. It was a building with a glass facade and the gym was on the second floor. The board on the top said cross fitness gym. Ayaan looked at it as he passed by, normally he wouldn't have glanced at it, but he was having so many dreams about this place. All the dreams were the same though, the same dream he had had the first time, with his father. He still couldn't figure out what he was trying to say. These dreams weren't just dreams Ayaan knew it, they were something more, the purpose was a little deep. But why this gym, was it because he had spent a lot of time here or was it something else. This gym was an essential part of his routine and life no doubt about that, probably that is why he was constantly remembering that. He hadn't gone to the gym in weeks, so probably his father was just asking him to go and start working out again. But that wasn't what Ayaan should be thinking, because that can wait, he needs to be prepared for something else, something worse.

Ayaan reached 10 minutes late, and as a result of that Milan and already arrived. Ayaan invited him in the car.

"Looks like it hasn't started yet" he said sitting in the car.

"There are two bouncers by the front gate and nobody seems to be in there."

"So we sit and wait until people start going in, and then we enter" Ayaan declared

So Ayaan and Milan had and old fashioned perfect stake out, like police officers usually do. What made it perfect was the fact that Milan had brought some really delicious samosas that his mother made tonight. Ayaan absolutely loved them. The skin was crunchy and crackling, the grease from the mutton inside dripping slightly after each bite, and the meat, the meat was perfectly done. Milan had brought a whole lot of them and Ayaan seemed to have had most of them. After the first five Ayaan lost count. But as Ayaan sat there eating those delicious delicacies, he examined the cathedral. It was just a glimpse what it used to be some 15 years ago. Ayaan remembered it, Ayaan had been in the cathedral when it was functioning as a church and holy place, not what it is now, and it was extravagant. 15 years ago this was the biggest church in the city probably one of the biggest in the country, but unfortunately it wasn't constructed to withstand one of the most gruesome acts of God. It was almost sad to believe the house of God was torn down by himself, but Ayaan wasn't going to question the lord's work. The church couldn't stand and 7.9 magnitude earthquake and most part of it crumpled like a piece of paper. It just didn't crumple though, it took 19 lives with it. Now what remained was just a broken building that was too expensive to renovate. Its architecture was inspired from the Vatican itself, and that's what made it so special, it was a church like no other. All that remained intact of the building was the front part with half a ceiling and courtyard in front of the entrance. It hadn't been maintained too so the exterior walls were black is it could be, it looked like the entire construction was made from coal bricks. There vines creeping in from all sides and wild plants growing over the compound walls and onto the road outside.

They had to wait for nearly an hour before the first man arrived the two guards in front looked at him and let him pass. Next two more men arrived with briefcase, probably carrying money and went inside. After that there was a whole line of people that followed. People of different heights, weights, class all went in the same and now it was time for Ayaan to do the same.

He got out of the car and Milan did the same. He locked the car and walked towards the building. The car was parked on the other side of the road, so he had to cross it. He saw the two security guards, and they saw him. They wore black shirts and black pants and had guns locked in their belts. Ayaan made sure he had his. Both had weirdly bushy moustaches and were alarmingly huge. Ayaan didn't bother making eye contact and quietly made his way to the entrance door of the cathedral. Ayaan could probably fight them if it came to it, he wasn't huge or had enormous upper body strength, but he had the skill. After all when would all his boxing training come to use and as his trainer used to say to him all the time "you don't have the muscle, but you have the heart, and that's the only muscle you need to worry about in a fight".

But it wasn't necessary at the moment, the guards didn't seem to be bothered about Ayaan getting in. Ayaan opened the main door to the cathedral, it opened quiet smoothly than Ayaan had expected. And the door opened to a great hall, which was long and with an enormous ceiling, part of which was now open to the sky. Ayaan was sincerely astonished to see what the hall consisted off. Clearly the hall was made for the church, it still had some of it left.

However most of the things were altered, the aisle was still present leading up to the altar where the several candles shun the room with light, but instead of the pews on either side of the aisle there consisted of round tables on which people sat playing cards. A candle was placed on each table and every player had a chair to sit on. The walls enclosing the room were decorated with brackets and picture frames. Ayaan got a glimpse of several of them at it was of the last supper and another was of the crucifixion. Ayaan also saw some that he didn't know which event it represented but certainly one that established the faith of Christianity.

He saw what was on the end of the aisle, and he saw a table, just before the altar, with two candles lit on either side. There was also a man sitting on the table, counting chips and Ayaan knew that he had without a doubt found his man. The man, presumably who Ayaan suspected him to be was surrounded by two other guards, kind of like the ones he saw on the outside. They had similar featured two, surprisingly so. Ayaan looked up just below the ceiling and saw the crucifix hanging from a partly broken wall, it seemed cracked but it hung comfortably. Ayaan started walking towards the end of the room, he didn't need to look back to ensure that Milan was following, the room was deadly silent and their footsteps were the only sound Ayaan could hear. The entire room had a very gloomy feeling to it, which made it even creepier.

Ayaan made his way to the table with the man seated on it, but was unsuccessful to do so. He was hindered in his path with one other guard that he never saw. Perhaps because the room had many dark corners and a man in an all-black clothing standing in a black corner is a tough spot. Ayaan looked around wondering how many people were hiding in all the dark spots in the room, a curious thought.

"Stop, where do you think you are headed" said the guard authoritatively.
But before Ayaan could explain to him the purpose of his visit and the person he was here to meet a voice came echoing through the room

"Let him come"
The guard gave way for Ayaan to see the source of the command, and it came right from the end of the hall, from the man sitting on the table.
The guard frisked Milan and then Ayaan only to discover his pistol hinged on his belt. He grabbed it, unclicked the holster and showed it to the man.

"Father, he is armed"

"Let him keep it, he won't trouble us" said the father, "will you Ayaan Shahi?"

CHAPTER EIGHT

Ayaan walked to the table at the end of the great hall with Milan right behind him. Ayaan got a chance to glimpse Milan's expression after the father called him by his name. The expression was confusion, shock, uncertainty but all pointed to the same question, how he knew my name".

Ayaan on the other hand was calm he knew this was coming as soon as he had heard the father's name from the stranger at the office. He knew the father that why he was so cautious about him, he needed to be, after what had happened in the past. He remembered it like it was yesterday, he received a phone call in the middle of the night, kind of like the phone call he received from Milan a few days back, but it wasn't that late in the night or early in the morning and Milan wasn't working for him at that time. Nevertheless he was hired for a case for a missing person, by a person named Peter Magya, who later Ayaan discovered also goes by the name "the father". Ayaan didn't know him well and took the case without any references, which he decided after to never do again. Somehow he had heard Ayaan's name and knew that he would have been perfect fit to his devious plans.

Ayaan was fresh and didn't know a lot about this city, and Peter, the name Ayaan knows him by, took advantage of that.

Somehow someway, Ayaan located the missing person, Ayaan didn't remember all the details, but he did remember what happened when the case was solved. However that was all in the past and Ayaan was hoping that it would not come up tonight.

Ayaan continued towards the table at the end of the church, Milan was right behind him. With every step he took he could feel the weapon attached to his belt. He knew how important it was at the moment, and how lucky he was to still have it with him.

It was a long room and the walk towards the end of it seemed longer. Ayaan glanced at the ceiling above him, or what was left of the ceiling. The water was seeping through the edges of the room, was it raining here? Ayaan wasn't sure, the sky was clear and filled with stars, the moon shun brighter than ever and moonlight was making the room look gloomy yet peaceful. God's blessing on the holy place perhaps. But the way it was being utilised right now, it may be god's wrath. The water coming from the ceiling could have easily been poison.

Ayaan was nearing the end of his walk and now the scene was much more vivid. He could see his face, the clean shaven, innocent and naive face which in truth was scarred, wretched and pure evil. Father was wearing a white shirt, neatly tucked in his pants, the sleeves were folded to his elbows and his massive hands were bare. Peter Magya was big man, no question about it, he probably ate food as much as Ayaan ate in 3 days in one sitting and still have space for Milan sized dessert. Two candles were lit on the table, all fresh, which meant Peter wasn't here for long. It was probably business time for Peter. Ayaan went towards the table and pulled up a chair and had a seat, Milan remained standing

"If it isn't Ayaan fucking Shahi, the best private investigator this city has seen in years", and the father spoke in deep voice. Ayaan kept silent despite of the profanity, it wasn't his turn to speak.

"and you must be his little sidekick, I have heard about" he continued. "What was your name?" He asked Milan. Milan didn't reply, he was still letting the whole situation sink in, but the father continued.

"Eh, fuck! I can't remember, it was a funny name".

Ayaan could see confused expression on Milan's face, he was angry because he had always been very sensitive about his first name and also perplexed as to how the person he had never encountered knew his name. But that what made Peter Magya aka the father so deadly dangerous. He had information about anything and everything going on in the city. He knew all the important people of this city and everything there was to know about them. He invested time and resources for this, he had spies and whistle blowers all around the city. He took time to memorize everything and remember it and it was a wise investment as it helped him in his line of work.

A man in a black suit came out of a dark corner of the room, Ayaan for all he could remember never even saw him approaching. He came closer to the table, leaned in on the other side and whispered something in peters ear. Peter set his gaze on Milan and gave small but sinister smirk.

"Ah, you are Chetak Milan now I remember". It seemed like he had to be reminded about it by his henchmen, but Ayaan decided against pointing it out to him in person.

"Son of ex inspector Hemant Milan, I knew your dad and he knew me very well, probably not from my current alias, but before, when I had just started in the business. He spent the last quarter of his career as an officer of the law on my case. He was an honest cop, that's why he never got around to catch me, he was an idiot"

Ayaan noticed Milan's fist clench, he was going to lose it Ayaan predicted, and he had to find a way to make sure this conversation doesn't turn into a brawl, or worse a massacre.

"He didn't get the idea of a catching a criminal, you see to catch one, you have to become one yourself. You can't hunt like the pack if you don't intend on becoming a wolf. It was good that your father retired with a little dignity or else I would have embarrassed real fucking bad."

Ayaan realized the intensity of the situation was starting to reach its boiling point, he would have to do something to cool it down. Milan was red, his teeth were clenched and he was sweating.

"Umm why don't you wait for me outside?" Ayaan requested Milan in a really politely.

For some odd reason, Milan understood the hidden urgency in his polite tone and obeyed. For another odd reason the father did too, he smirked and looked away to the gambling tables situated in the church.

It took some time even after Milan had walked through the long passage leading to the exit and left the building, for Ayaan to be confident enough to start asking questions again. They had been in this building for nearly 20 minutes and haven't even got the chance to express the reason they were here.

"He doesn't know our history does he?" The father spoke before Ayaan could frame his questions.

"No" Ayaan replied
Ayaan had feared this topic might be discussed, he really wanted to avoid that.

"It is not that big deal anyway, I don't know why you felt and still feel upset about it, so many years later"
This was only half true, because it was a big deal and Ayaan was getting frustrated and angry at the fact of how little that incident meant to the father.
"

You asked me to search a man just so that after I had located him you could kill him" Ayaan tried to suppress his anger.

"Yes and I paid you enough for that"
Ayaan banged his hand on the table hard

"That's beside the point, you cut him into seven pieces, and it took the cops a week just to identify the body"

The guards now we're standing close to the table now, probably try were expecting Ayaan to do something rash.
Peter put his hand up in the air as a gesture for the guards to stand down.

"what's done is done" he said calmly, he didn't even seem affected by Ayaan's tone. "And you promised me never to see me again and asked me never to contact you again, then why the hell are you here?"

"Information, I need information about someone and I think you have what I need"

"Oh yeah?"

Peter was going to say something else but he was cut off by the commotion at one of the gambling tables in the room.

Two of the guards dressed in all black dragged a man towards the table where Ayaan was seated. The man was skinny and had light French beard that didn't really fit his face. He was without a doubt drunk, Ayaan was sure about that, his eyes showed that evidently. The two guards had his both hands locked and he was trying hard to escape.

"He was caught cheating father" said one of the guards. It still astonished Ayaan how everyone referred to Peter as the father.

Peter got up from his chair and walked towards the man. He unbuttoned his cuffs, folded his shirt to his elbows and stood face to face with the man. He tilted his head sideways and looked at the man from head to toe. Next, everything happened very fast. Peter threw two mighty blows to the man's face followed by a huge head-butt. The man was bleeding and bleeding bad. His lips were torn his jaw was fractured Ayaan assumed and his nose was bleeding like a faucet. Peter grabbed his jaw and pulled him up.

"You see this" he pointed towards the crucifix, "God is watching and God doesn't appreciate when you cheat at blackjack"

He threw another punch with his right hand, this time Ayaan could hear his jaw crack.

"You don't cheat with God in his own home" he continued, "If I see you ever again, I am going to send you straight to God himself"

He gave his last blow to the gut of the man and the

guards dragged him out.

The man had lost all conciseness, Ayaan was afraid on if the man was in need for any medical attention. But Ayaan could do nothing at the moment and the man was stupid if he thought he could outsmart Peter Magya, he should have known better.

Peter walked back to the table and took his seat.

From the light of the burning candles on the table Ayaan could see the fire in Peter's eyes, it wasn't the fire of anger but the same fire he had seen seven years ago, the fire of satisfaction. This man strived to hurt people. He had learnt it the hard way seven years and that's also when Ayaan had learnt that there are two kinds of victims in the world. One who actually are victims due to other people's actions and are completely innocent, and second who are victims because of their own actions and deserve to be in the place they are. It was an important life lesson for Ayaan he had learnt that not everyone who is in trouble is a victim, maybe its justice. Ayaan would have given anything to go back in time and not find the man who went missing, maybe that would have saved a lot of people from a lot of grief including him.

After witnessing the beating Peter just gave the gambler, Ayaan realized he would have to stand up and speak his mind and confront this man, or he will just intimidate and dominate him. Ayaan decided to do just that, he will have to take control of this conversation if he intended to make any progress towards solving the case.

"You are a funny man Peter" Ayaan said.
Peter was pretty taken aback by this, probably because he didn't expect Ayaan to call him by his first name.

"Your father was the kindest and most pious man I had ever met, look what you have created in his name"
Ayaan thought this might piss the father off, but instead Peter just smiled.

"You are a funny man Ayaan, you talk to me about doing wrong things in the name of my father in the name of God? While you have never even been sure of who your God was for the most part of your life"
Ayaan silently listened

"I still remember I was here working at this very church on a Sunday morning, some 25 years ago. Everyone was seated and the prayers were going on, and in comes some 13 year old boy, with a Muslim cap on his head and dressed like a true Muslim would have. Everybody were surprised to see that boy, but that boy was a tough son of a bitch, because he didn't mind, he came in lit some candles asked for the priest, my father. You know who that boy was Ayaan Shahi? It was you, and I know you visited temples and all sorts of other places after your father passed away. People said you had lost it, that maybe you needed medical care, so don't come up to me and tell me that I screwed over my father and my god, you have no idea what it's like to be a son of a religious man and never really be able to live up to his or others expectations."
The fact was, Ayaan did know what it was like to be a son of pious man, for all Ayaan could remember his father was a really religious man. Had a great reputation and respect amongst his community, but of course he did not live long enough to thrust it all on Ayaan.

"But you certainly aren't here to talk about my faith? So tell me Ayaan what are you really here for?"
This was his opportunity to turn this conversation back

on course and Ayaan decided to take it.

"I am here to discuss a murder" Ayaan wanted to start off with strongly. Ayaan waited for peters reaction, but he didn't get it instead he got the fathers reaction. Ayaan saw him get his pistol out and place it on the table. The gesture was clearly a warning, beware what you say.

Ayaan cleared his throat, he had to finish what he had to say.

"And I have been assigned to this case, the victim was shot in his office and his name is Mr. Agarwal" Ayaan didn't meet his eyes while saying all this and left out the fact that he didn't even know the victims first name.

It seemed as if someone had taken two tennis balls and placed it in the father's eye sockets. He was shocked, clearly he was hearing about it for the first time. It was astonishing that man who has information about possibly every important man of the city has no clue about this man or even the incident.

Ayaan was expecting a ' no fucking way' kind of a reaction but all he got was laughter. After digesting the entire situation Peter burst out laughing. His laughter was soft but seemed genuine and that got Ayaan pretty confused.

"Honestly speaking" Peter said after he had controlled his laughter," I was expecting a whole different situation when you mentioned murder"

It became evident to Ayaan that he was very lucky to have not been assigned to the other case Peter was referring to. That would have ended really badly for Ayaan.

"So now that we have got that clear" Ayaan said with a much more confident voice," let's talk about the murder, where were you exactly when it happened and by that I mean the Friday night?"

A typical interrogation question, kind of like they ask on those idiotic crime investigation series that come on television. But Ayaan had no choice but to ask it.

"So you actually suspect that I might be behind this murder?" Peter asked

He laughed again this time a little louder, the question was indeed a rhetorical one. "Do you even know what kind of person your victim was?" It was another rhetorical question, but Ayaan felt the urge to actually confess that in truth he did not really know anything about his victim but he resisted it. He wanted to know what Peter knew about him, although his reaction to this entire situation was inclining Ayaan to think that probably Peter wasn't behind all of this, but it is better not to scratch his name of the list just yet, even though his name is the only one on the list.

"I loved the guy, he was one of my regulars" Peter said.

"Regulars at gambling?" Ayaan was curious, if he was a regular here at the table, did he too get beat down like the man did just a few minutes ago. If he can do this to people who doesn't know, God knows what he does to people he knows and finds out they have been cheating.

"Oh no no, not gambling, Agarwal was never a gambler, but that son of a bitch sure liked getting high a lot"

"High? You mean marijuana?" Ayaan was familiar with the concept although he had never tried it"

"You are wrong again Ayaan Shahi, I meant cocaine" he said the word cocaine a little more softly that the others, it almost nice to see that even a person like the father was conscience of what he was saying.

"Cocaine!?" Ayaan was amazed and the amazement was reflected in his voice.

"Oh yes, that man was a crack head, couldn't go a day without it"
That was a new discovery, something Ayaan hadn't even thought about and Ayaan sure would think a lot. Ayaan took some time to let it sink in.

"You see these bags" Peter pointed to his left. "Those are this month's stock, and the seventh of every month, I would wait at this very table and Agarwal would come in and buy all of it"

"All of it?"

"Oh yeah all of it, this is a stock I buy to supply to the whole city and this guy buys all of it, one man. I would smuggle more but I can't"

Ayaan listened intently he could hear the frustration in peters voice at that last remark, he couldn't stand that a man like him even had limitations

"I got concerned that this guy might actually die of consuming so much, so I had him followed for a week. But it turned out he was fit and fine even after consuming grade A product like this one" he gestured to the bags again. " we never knew his first name all the time he had been coming here, but we just called him the dragon, dragon Agarwal"

This valuable information for Ayaan, he finally thought he might have something to solve this case. Maybe Agarwal didn't just buy cocaine from him, maybe he had someone else too and maybe he might have gotten into trouble with that guy.

"You know I have heard rumors that he owed you a great amount of debt?" Ayaan questioned politely. He was positive now that Peter might actually be innocent for once.

"So he was a little late, it's not like this was the first time. He was sometimes late to pay but he always paid at the end. He was my biggest customer I wouldn't do anything to ruin that. I am not a monster"

Oh but Ayaan had seen the monster inside this man, and it was terrifying.

Now all Ayaan required was a push to get his case on the right track.

"So you know where Mr. Agarwal lives?"

"Oh yes I do" he replied calmly," do you require his address"

Now Ayaan was in a tough situation, if he said yes then he would appear needy and Peter loves to take advantage of the needy. Ayaan was fortunate enough to get such a lot of information out of him without any issues. But now it seemed the good times were over, his luck had finally run out.

"No I don't need it, I was just curious" Ayaan lied.

"Oh that's sad, I would have loved to help you out more, I really liked that guy and would love to see him get justice"

"Sweet words from a bitter mouth" Ayaan thought. He never for a second beloved anything he just said, it was foolish to think that a man like him was capable of compassion.

"I think I should be leaving, it's getting late" Ayaan got up from the chair.

"Well it's always nice meeting you Ayaan Shahi, whenever we meet we discover something new about each other"

Well that was partly true Ayaan thought, he did discovers the new lows this man could go to.

Peter reached under his table and brought up a cola can and opened it. It took Ayaan a while to understand that it was actually a beer can. Ayaan was disgusted to be honest, not because he was against people consuming alcohol, he had friends who did that and he was completely alright with it even though he never had a drink. But he was disgusted with the fact that the man sitting in front of him carried the legacy of such a holy man and was currently responsible for the holy place they were currently standing inside. He had clearly disregarded and disrespected his father and the thing he cared for most, the church in one instant and that didn't sit well with Ayaan.

"Oh I knew you didn't drink that's why I never bothered offering it to you, but do you want it" he had clearly understood Ayaan's expressions.

Ayaan looked at the crucifix behind the table, Peter turned too.

"Oh don't worry about him" Peter continued "he only drinks wine, beer makes him gassy" he laughed hysterically.

Ayaan had had it with him, he couldn't take it anymore, and he turned and made his way to the exit.

As he was on his way to the exit, he heard Peter yell at the top of his voice, such that everyone in the room could here.

"When are you ever going to gather up the guts to kick my ass?"

Ayaan could imagine the smile Peter might have had, but he never turned to confirm it. Everyone on the cards table was looking at him now as he made his way to the door. His fists were clenched but his mind was still thinking rationally. He opened the door of the church and went out.

CHAPTER NINE

Milan was standing by the gate of the church, looking on towards the road. He had a cigarette in his right hand and it was lit. He didn't notice Ayaan exit the building or even when Ayaan started walking towards him. He took a puff and turned. His reactions quick, he quickly dropped the cigarette and stubbed it out with his foot. Ayaan wasn't surprised at all by this reaction. He knew that Milan smoked now and then and Ayaan also knew why. He always had a smoke whenever he was feeling a very strong emotion whether it was despair or anger. He always went for a smoke whenever he wanted to escape his thoughts, it was merely a stress buster for him and that is the reason Ayaan didn't mind it. Although it was a little surprising to see Milan smoking right now, it could only lead to one explanation, Peter really got to him. He really must have struck a nerve.

Ayaan walked where Milan was standing and started talking. He described everything that happened inside the building after he left.

He even asked him to call Dr. Anand at the morgue and ask him to check the body for any narcotic. Although it didn't seem necessary, if it were there Dr. Anand would have found it regardless of Ayaan asking him. Nevertheless Ayaan thought it was a formality he should make. Ayaan was beat, he already had a long day and now it was prolonged by a really stressful night. He walked towards his car, got in and drove back to the apartment. There were very few cars on the road and the ride back was peaceful. This gave Ayaan the chance to reflect upon what happened in the church a while ago. Was he too quick to judge, was he jumping to conclusions without seeing the bigger picture? Ayaan doubted his actions. Maybe Peter did care about Mr. Agarwal, maybe he was willing to help and just help without him having any ulterior motives. Probably Ayaan should have given him the benefit of the doubt, but his experience with the man had taught him a lesson he couldn't forget and after all experience is the best teacher.

Ayaan reached his apartment and parked his car. He went to the elevator, surprisingly it was already on the ground floor, but Ayaan wanted to stretch his legs a little more, he decided to climb the stairs. It was a long and slow climb, but Ayaan didn't mind it this time, it was something that Ayaan wanted to do. He had the house keys so there was no need to knock and ring the doorbell, he knew everyone inside would be fast asleep. He unlocked the door and dragged himself to the sofa. The room was dimly lit, giving it a gloomy yet cozy feel to it. The windows on the right were wide open and the wind was howling in, the curtains reflected the winds intensity. It was cool and comfortable and Ayaan didn't want to go to his room, it seemed very far away and Ayaan couldn't muster the energy to get up from the sofa. He kicked off his shoes and straightened his legs and spread his body completely on the sofa. The lights were dim and looked like little fireflies in the room, he was tired very tired. He shut his eyes

He arrived at the coined cathedral again, only this time he was alone and this time he had no gun. How he got there was a question Ayaans subconscious didn't want answered, but since he didn't see his car nearby he eliminated that option indefinitely. He was on the side of the road and in front of him stood the great church. It wasn't like Ayaan

84

thought it would be, he had just visited it looked dark and probably haunted, but not this place it was marble white and beautiful as it could ever have been. The road was empty and the gates of the church were opened, looked like Ayaan had only one way to proceed. Ayaan made his way to the church, he felt fresh which was completely opposite to the way he was feeling when he fell asleep.

It was surprising that Ayaan remembered falling asleep and the fact that he was dreaming. He felt he could wake up if he wanted to, he could at least try, but the thing was Ayaan didn't want to wake up. He wanted to explore this world his mind had created for him, he wanted to know what comes next.

He pushed open the front door to the church and inside was something Ayaan never imagined. There were lights and candles all around the room, the roof was covered and the walls were decorated. You could see paintings depicting the last supper and the crucifixion on each side of the aisle, they all were framed and preserved well. The altar was lit with nearly 100 candles if not more. However the room was still empty, there was no one in sight. Ayaan proceeded to the far end of the room, he saw the crucifix hanging and as he walked he saw all pews on each side, perfect wooden finish, clean with no signs of dust but with no sign of humans as well. Ayaan reached the last pew, actually first from the altar and to his astonishment he saw a man sitting there, waiting. Could this be? Why was he here again did he have something to say again. All this questions were filling Ayaans head as once again he saw his father sitting and waiting for him.

Ayaan stood staring at his father, but his father never glanced to see his son standing right next to him. It was so unlike the dream he had before, this time his father didn't even try to talk to him. He sat ideally gazing at the burning candles. Ayaan wanted to say something, yell and scream, he wanted to know why his father was here, what was he trying to communicate, but he had no control over his body. He just stood there like a statue and hoped for something to happen. And something did, but it certainly took its time. Ayaans father got up from his seat and went to altar table, he didn't pray or lit any of the candles, and he just stared at the crucifix of Jesus Christ. After that he turned towards Ayaan, and smiled, like he always did when he saw Ayaan confused or befuddled. He walked towards Ayaan and then walked past him. Ayaan stood there and witnessed his father leave the church. What now? Ayaan wondered, should he have followed him or should he wait, waiting seemed to be the right way to go. He decided to have a seat, he went to the seat his father was seated on, but instead of an empty chair he found a note. The note was a white paper neatly folded, all Ayaan had to do was open it and read what his father wanted him to know. He opened the first fold, then the second and just as when he was about to open the third and final fold of the paper something else opened and he was back in the living room of his apartment.

There were a lot of things happening in the room, the television was playing some sort of a cartoon movie, Salma was chasing Ayman through the room with a school bag in her right hand, yelling in the process.

"Come on Ayman, you are getting late for school. The rickshaw will be here in no time"

"I don't want to go to school"

"Ayman!"

"No!"

"Ayman come on good girl"

"No no!"

This went on for quite some time. It took Ayaan quite some time to analyze and understand the situation. He felt tired and sleepy. By the time Ayaan was sitting up on the sofa, he found his daughter seated on the dining table and quietly but reluctantly having breakfast. Salma Was feeding her and Ayman was gulping. She was hungry without a doubt. Ayaan recalled having dinner with Ayman last night before he headed out for his case. Did Ayman eat her full last night? Ayaan was not sure, he had a lot of things on his mind at that time, and so is it possible that the concern of his daughter having a proper dinner eluded him? The thought struck him like a bolt of lightning. It was worrying for sure, not the fact that Ayman didn't have proper food, she was moody and it was probably just a phase, but the worrying part was that he was too distracted to care. This was probably the first time this had happened, ever since Maya, his wife had passed away, he had had to perform a double role of both parents. Sure Salma had helped him out with maintaining the house, but she was never a mother to Ayman, it was always him... Always. Ayman had already been disappointed with the fact that Ayaan didn't allow him to participate in the play, so it was Ayaans job right now to make sure that he was there for her when she felt down. It was his responsibility.

Ayaan got up from the sofa and went to the dining table. He pulled up a chair and sat next to Ayman. Salma was still feeding her and she was still eating. It was an omelet drenched in butter and bread to go with it. It was what Ayaan just wanted, his stomach was curling, it was only time till it started making sounds. He checked the clock on the wall in front of him, it read 7 25.

It took a couple of minutes for Ayman to finish her breakfast, after which she got ready and headed downstairs with Salma behind her. There were a lot of things on the dining table Ayaan noticed. A fruit basket, an empty yet dirty plate Ayman had left behind, newspaper and also a small parchment, folded neatly. Ayaan couldn't help but wonder what was inside it, he reached out and grabbed it. After unfolding it he realized it was something he had already gone through before. It was the consent letter from Ayaan's School, with the space where the parent's signature required still empty. Ayaan was still hung up on the fact that his daughter deserved a better role than what she was offered. Ayaan wanted to throw it away, but right now putting it aside would do. He grabbed the newspaper, it felt fresh, and the smell was pungent and refreshing. There was nothing like an early morning read of the newspaper. Well to be fair there is nothing like reading anything in the morning. Ayaan scanned through newspaper, the front page never had anything of Ayaans interest, for quite some time cricket and one of its tournaments which going on was the only thing news worthy in this country at the moment. Ayaan never bothered with that sport, he felt it was tedious and mundane. 5 days to decide a winner and that to not certain if there will be a winner, more formats than the countries that participated and rules that read longer than the pitch itself. Ayaan always beloved that sports were a way to escape your life for a certain time, but this sport had become life and that was something Ayaan didn't agree with. Although Ayaan enjoyed a pleasant morning read, his main purpose for reading the paper was to see if the case he had been working on had made it to the papers yet, it was definitely high time.

After scanning through the paper thrice, making sure that he had gone through every article, Ayaan concluded that the case had still not made it to the paper and it seemed like it wasn't on any other media as well. The paper contained articles about pot holes on the streets and dog shows in the city, but people and murders were something the writers didn't find intriguing. But was it the writers to blame or just the whole situation Ayaan had on his hands. Nobody was really bothered about this murder, except for a pretentious thug who had lied and cheated to get to the top and here was Ayaan losing thoughts and sleep over this case. He was even having nightmares because of the case.

Ayaans dreams were getting more and more interesting. His dreams were not merely dreams or a projection of his subconscious it was something more. Ayaan remembered his mother telling this to him when he was young. His mother believed that when a person goes to sleep he doesn't just sleep, but dies. His soul is taken from his body and taken to heaven and then blown back to him when he wakes up. Ayaan hadn't given it much thought, firstly because he was too young to understand the meaning of it and secondly he knew his mother to keep really very superstitious beliefs. Some of them were really very bizarre, but some were true as well. Ayaan was more of a skeptic, so it was always hard for him to believe anything just for the sake of believing it, he had to ask questions. And that was something Ayaan encouraged everyone to do whether it was Milan or Ayman. He liked it when people questioned matters of religious beliefs and practices, it indicated that they really wanted to know what they believe in.

Will he have to eventually go to the person who can really help him out with this, Ayaan wasn't sure, he would love to avoid that. And probably this was just a phase so it might just pass and he would be alright again.

The door of the apartment swung open and in came Salma, but without Ayman this time. Clearly she had dropped her off and she was on her way to school. But Ayaan couldn't resist he had to ask just for the sake of asking.

"Did you drop of Ayman properly?"

"Yes" came the reply, "she really didn't want to go to school"

"Did you ask why?"

"Yeah, she kept on saying that all her friends were part of some play and she wanted to be but now she isn't and that's why she would like to avoid school"

That was odd, Ayaan was confident that his daughter was content with the decision he made regarding the play. Then why was she behaving this way. Was she not telling him something but that was not like Ayman, she was straight forward and open about her feelings, especially to her own father. He would have to talk to her about this later. Ayaan was so involved in his own thoughts that he completely neglected the fact that Salma was still standing in front of him, waiting to answer any further questions he might have.

"You can go now" Ayaan permitted

"Okay, would like to have breakfast?"

"Yes" Ayaan did feel hungry

"The regular?"

"Yes" Ayaan replied, because something's should never change.

Ayaan had his whole day planned out. He had to work in the case without a doubt, he still had no information that could lead him in the right direction. So he had decided that today he was going to go to the Mr. Agarwal's office again, in the hope of finding more clues. You can't visit the crime scene enough, that's what Ayaan was taught when he started off as a private investigator, so he had to go back in order to move forward. He thought he might go a little late this time, possibly at the time of lunch when everyone had some time to spare. If Ayaan was lucky he might get another tip like he did from the stranger at office on his last visit there. Hope and determination is what was required now, Ayaan knew and he was willing to give it all he got.

CHAPTER TEN

The heat was burning and the light blinding. If Ayaan hadn't been in his car and the air conditioning hadn't been on, it could have been very difficult for him indeed. He saw around him, the mirrors showed less, but he could vividly see what was happening in front of him. He was in the middle of a traffic jam, with three cars visibly in front of him, two busses and numerous scooters and rickshaws. It was unbelievable how much people cared about reaching some place and how little they cared about others on the way. Life had become fast and hectic for the people in this city. It wasn't their fault, the city had changed. People had to get rich and get rich fast, they had to buy things even they didn't know exist and everything should happen as fast as it can. It wasn't so long ago

Ayaan remembered when the city was at peace. Sure there were a lot less people living in it, but still it was not so hectic. It took nearly half an hour for the traffic to clear, by then probably the lunch at the office would have already started.

Ayaan was surely going to be late and he hated that. He hated when people didn't respect time and its value, now it was him. He didn't do it on purpose for sure, but he still couldn't help but feel a little guilty. He reached the Olympus building and found Milan's scooter parked in front. He parked his car right behind the scooter and made his way to the building. The heat was unbearable and Ayaan was neither wearing sunglasses nor a cap. He had to keep his hand over his eyes to stop himself from getting blinded. He looked both ways of the street, it was dead empty. No soul wanted to burn in this kind of hell. There were a few trees on the street, few was an overestimation, Ayaan counted three. They were swaying from the hot air, like they were unaffected by the heat. Ayaan went through the sliding door, he felt like he could stay in here forever. The air conditioning was a blessing. He stood his ground for a moment to recover. His eyes took several seconds to adjust to the dull yet cozy room of the building. In the corridor leading up to the elevator he found Milan standing and waiting.

"I was just about to call you sir "he started.

Ayaan was about to reply when he realized that his tongue was as dry as the dessert, all he could do was gesture to Milan with his hands that he needed water.

They were in the elevator and it was set to stop on the third floor. Ayaan wasn't stopped at the reception this time and so he didn't have to have another idiotic conversation with the lady who knew nothing. It looked like the lunch break was already in progress, Ayaan believed that this would make his task a lot simpler to achieve. His task was still the same when he first walked out of the very same building he was now inside, information, any valuable information. This investigation had turned into a farce and it was a bad one as it was miles from being funny.

The elevator came to a halt on the third floor and its door opened wide. Ayaan entered an empty hallway, nothing but cubicles were in sight with empty chairs left in a random pattern. Ayaan had to find someone and talk, but the only sound audible to Ayaan was Milan's slow breathing and the sound of the air conditioners cooling the room.

Ayaan saw the office at the end of the room where it all started. The curtains were wide open and he could see everything what was happening on the inside. The leather chair on which he had found Mr. Agarwal was empty and pointed towards the desk. The desk was just as it had been on the day of the crime. It was shocking how nothing in office was displaced after the crime, not even the people's emotions. How a person could have such little impact on the people around him was the question that lured in Ayaans mind. Nevertheless he was given a task that he had to accomplish, it was never his job to ask what and why, he had to concentrate on the 'who' and the 'how'.

Ayaan made his way towards the pantry, as he made his way towards the room, he could hear voices, and some were cheers also. The passageway to the pantry was narrow and dimly lit, but Ayaan's mind was filling with possibilities and curiosity of what he was about to witness. Ayaan made it to the opening and could see the pantry, it was a small room, and it looked even smaller when it was filled with 12 people. Nobody saw Ayaan as they all were seated on stools with their back to the entrance where Ayaan and Milan were standing. 12 grown men were sitting and staring at a big white sheet pinned up on the wall in front of them. All of them wore white shirts, tucked in to black or brown pants finished with a variety of ties. A man wearing a red tie got up and faced all the other men.

"So let me hear all the bets" he said excited.
There were some cheers.

"So who thinks Gandhi did it?"
Several hands shot up

"Alright let me remind you the betting starts at 500, so if you can't pay up don't bet." He pointed to a short man seated in the front row wearing a black tie.

"Let me have it folks, any other suspects? Who could have killed me Agarwal?"

Ayaan's jaw dropped. These people were actually betting on the case, Ayaan was lost for words.

Ayaan heard someone say the father and several nodding heads to that name. Several other names popped up as well, names Ayaan knew were upper level office employees. Someone even better that the case would never be solved. At the end of what seemed like a really long 10 minutes, the white sheet was filled with name of the suspects and people who betted on them to be the murderer. The amount of money people put in it were outstanding.

The 10 minutes Ayaan stood there, his emotions went from being thoroughly shocked to his core to being furiously angry.

Without saying a single word Ayaan marched inside the room, made his way to the pinned up sheet, pulled it down and tore it to pieces. He could feel the excitement die out and turn into confusion. He was sure everybody knew who he was because nobody dared to raise his voice in front of him. All the frustration of the case came out on the sheet of paper. Ayaan wasn't thinking straight, but thinking straight hadn't gotten him anywhere in the case, so it was about time to do something extreme. Ayaan saw faces staring at him, dumb founded. Ayaan knew that he wasn't going to get anything out of these people, he wasn't even slightly hopeful, so he had different plan.

"I want to meet your manager, Praveen Gandhi"

It was time for Ayaan to find out what was really going on in this office

"It's on the fourth floor, first office to the right" said the man in the red tie.

The room was silent and the eyes were still on Ayaan when Ayaan left the room. Ayaan took long strides back to the hall way and straight to the elevator door, Milan at his heels. The elevator door opened at the fourth floor, this floor was completely different from the floor below. This one looked like a corridor of a luxurious hotel. The hallway was dimly lit but had a pleasant ambience, there was carpet all the way on the floor and it was chilling. Ayaan took the right and ended up at the office. The door read ' Praveen Gandhi marketing manager', Ayaan knocked the door twice and then opened it.

The room interior was as impressive as the floor itself, ample space, and comfortable sofas at one end of the office and a finely polished desk with a huge chair at the other side of it. On them at chair sat a man that was just as Ayaan remembered him. The moustache on the face was thick and the hair on his head was jet black. He was in a middle of a conversation on his phone, Ayaan shut the office door, harder than he intended it. The door slammed hard and Praveen Gandhi looked over to Ayaan.

"Yes?! How may I help you?"

"Alright what the hell is going on here?" Ayaan questioned authoritatively

"I am sorry who are you?"

"I am Ayaan" said Ayaan disgusted now

His eyes glowed as he recognized Ayaan.

"Oh yes of course, please have a seat Mr. Shahi"
He kept his phone aside and gestured Ayaan to have a seat.
Ayaan obliged.

"Okay, I have to get something straight with you" Ayaan
started calming down a little. "Don't you want this case to be
solved and Mr. Agarwal to justice?"

"Of course we do, he was loved and respected by ever..."

"Okay that is not even a little true" Ayaan interrupted. "If
you or anyone genuinely cared for Mr. Agarwal, I wouldn't
be here. I don't think you know this, but just a floor below
there are people betting on this case, putting money on who
turns out to be the murderer. And I am afraid to say but you
are on the betting list."
He just smiled through his thick moustache.

"So they are making this a little interesting for themselves,
shouldn't hinder your investigation."

"I am not solving a case where I am the only one
concerned about getting the guilty to justice, so you better
tell me what's going on around here, or I am dropping this
case for good"
Praveen Gandhi sighed.

"Fine if you have to know, the reason why nobody cares
about this case as much is because in truth Mr. Agarwal
wasn't the best of people."

Ayaan predicted as much.

"He was very infamous for all his habits and his interests. I mean you visited the church where he frequently visited, you know what kind of people he was involved with, and that is not something people look up to in our society.

This was not news for Ayaan, he had thought about all of this as soon as he found out about the father and his relationship with Mr. Agarwal. Clearly if a man is liked by the likes of Peter Magya he couldn't be a very pleasant man. But Ayaan still waited.

"He was an addict as well"

"I know, he abused drugs, and what else do you know"

"Oh no, not drugs, he you know was really into women, if you know what I mean" he smiled uncomfortably
Ayaan digested that, but Ayaan didn't quite know what he meant.

"So he was a womanizer? I wouldn't call it addiction"

"No I meant women in a… you know sexual persuasion, if you know what I mean."

Now Ayaan did, and he was astounded greatly. In all seriousness Ayaan didn't think of Mr. Agarwal as a hedonist.

"He had affairs, with a lot of women. I know it is hard to imagine for you, but trust me if he was alive you wouldn't have liked him. It is commendable that you take your job so seriously and you are so ambitious to solve this case that you came through despite interest and patience, but I strongly feel that some people are meant to die alone, miserable and without reason. Their whole life being an incomplete story, similar to the one we are in right now."

CHAPTER ELEVEN

"What are we going to do now" this question was on Ayaan's mind ever since he had walked out of the office and finally Milan found his voice to ask that question. And now that the question was asked Ayaan was still pondering over on what the answer could be. This case made absolutely no sense whatsoever, there was no link, no suspects, no witnesses and not even a single person willing to help. The only person Ayaan could recall being grief stricken by the death of Mr. Agarwal was his Coke dealer, and that too because he had lost his most faithful customer. Ayaan had never given up a case in his career, he felt it was his responsibility to bring justice and peace to the people, but now it seemed that the people had made their peace with injustice.

"I have no idea" Ayaan sighed.

They were in the reception area on the ground floor, overlooking the door that led to the outside.

The door had the picture of the earth and the message that read "you are entering a different world. Ayaan thought it was absurd, the world on the inside was no different from what was on the outside. Ayaan had realized that, the same carelessness, the same selfish acts and the same attitude towards society and its people. It was the harsh reality and it was unpleasant.

Ayaan's cellphone rang just when they were about to exit the building. He decided to remain indoors and answer it, it looked pretty hot still on the outside and the inside was cool and comfortable. The phone was from commissioner Vishnu, Ayaan hesitated but answered it eventually.

"Ayaan my boy! How are you?!" Said a thick enthusiastic voice.

Ayaan never understood the reason why the commissioner referred to him as boy, he was hardly 5 years elder to him. Although he was one of the youngest commissioner in this city, but everybody knew how he had gotten to that post so young. He had taken the low road, and had helps from many people who were successful by taking the similar road.

"I am great sir, how are you"

"Ayaan I need to see you, come at my office at around 7, alright?" He said authoritatively.

There was no getting out of this, Ayaan was absolutely sure.

"Sure sir" he replied
And the conversation ended, without even saying goodbye.

"Who was it sir" Milan asked curiously

"Vishnu"

"The commissioner?"

Ayaan nodded, "He has called me to his office in the evening"

"You want me to come"

"No I don't think you should, it will be better if I go by myself"

Milan didn't insist, Ayaan could see that he was relieved he didn't have to come.

Dreams are reality of the mind. They are an abstract composition of thoughts of the mind. Dreams express what the mind possess. This was the scientific side of what Ayaan believed his dreams about his father meant. While his spiritual side believed them to be a deeper than just projections of his thoughts. He had a dream again where his father had visited him, but this time it wasn't in the gym or the church, it was a place Ayaan couldn't remember very well, or perhaps he just didn't want to. The only thing significant about the scene was six inches below his eyes. Blood was pouring out of his left chest, with a bullet hole. Whoever fired it must have aimed for his heart, Ayaan knew who might have fired it, Ayaan knew this scenario before but why was he in it again. The pain was blinding, it was impossible to get used to, especially when he was dripping blood and making a pool around where he was seated. A man, his father walked towards him, right when Ayaan was expecting his actual savior. He walked slowly, Ayaan was sweating and panting and the only words he could muster were "help me father"

His father leaned over him and crouched to meet his eye. He smiled like he always did and shook his head.
Ayaan's eyes widened out of shock

"But... But you are my fa... Father, who else will save me?"

Ayaan could feel his legs and hands stop moving
His father smiled again, it was dark and the moon sparklers in his eyes. He pointed his index finger towards Ayaan.

"Me?! How?" These were surely the last words Ayaan would say.

His father leaned closer and closer, so much that his lips were just an inch away from Ayaan's right ear and he whispered
"Rediscover what's within"

Ayaan woke up startled. He was on his sofa in his living room and Ayman was seated in front of the television screen, fixed watching some cartoon. Ayaan rubbed his eyes, and put his feet down on the ground. The clock read 6:16. Ayaan had slept quite a lot and he had dreamed of his father again, only this time his father spoke to him. What he meant by those words was something Ayaan had to figure out.
Rediscover what's within

Ayaan had to be going to the police station soon, he had a meeting with the commissioner and he couldn't afford to miss that.

He had an early dinner by himself while his daughter was still fixated in front of the TV. He watched his daughter giggle and smile watching her favorite shows as he was served with hot food at the dining table.

Hunger was discovered within.

He barely ate, he shoved food down his throat, and he hardly tasted it. Spoonful after spoonful, he never realized how hungry he was.

He finished eating in under 10 minutes and then got fresh. He kissed his daughter good night as he might be late and his daughter might have fallen asleep.

He quickly pressed the button on the elevator and surprisingly the elevator opened its doors for Ayaan to enter. He pressed for the ground floor and headed out as soon as the doors swing open again.

A rush of energy was discovered within.

His head was crowded with thoughts and scenarios that could occur when he reached the police station. None of them were pleasant.

Ayaan drove his car out of his building and onto the road that lead to his destination. He saw his gym again, he realized he had not been going there for some time now, his fitness was important to him, he had to start over again and Ayaan hated that.

The clock in Ayaan's car read 7:12, Ayaan was late, and he shouldn't have been.
He rushed out of the car and checked his phone for the time, it showed 6:49.

Tranquility was discovered within.

He sighed and walked towards the police station.

Through the main door, enter the main hall take the first door on the right and then the door at the end of the passageway and he was in commissioner Vishnu's office, this was something Ayaan knew and was prepared for, but the thing that he did not anticipate was the amount of people in the main hall. The room was suffocating and smelled. Several people bumped into Ayaan on their way out, one person bumped so hard that he fell on the floor along with whole bunch of papers, he quickly started to gather all of the papers as they flew all across the room. Ayaan would have helped but he had an appointment. He went to one of the police officers sitting on the desk.

"Is the commissioner here, I am Ayaan Shahi, investigating the Agarwal case"

The officer didn't bother to look up from his desk, he just pointed to his right as he fiddled with his mobile phone. Ayaan knew the way of course, he wanted to be polite, he had forgotten that the gesture is not recognized in a place like this. He walked through and reached the office door. The air smelt a little better but still the tobacco and cigarette was potent.

He knocked once and opened the door.

The office was a large room, with a big desk at one end surrounded by chairs and a sofa at the opposite end. He saw commissioner Vishnu focused on his laptop. The laptop was placed on the desk. He must have been doing something important, he had frowns on his forehead, it seemed as if he was trying to decide something encrypted.

"Sir!" Ayaan coughed.
He looked up.

"Ah Ayaan my boy, have a seat"

He gestured to a seat right in front of him. Ayaan sat down. The commissioner was still busy on his laptop. Ayaan took the time to examine the room he was in. It was a pretty big office, with the walls painted yellow and green. The emblem for the police force hung behind the commissioner's chair, just above a small mantel with lots of trophies and medals. The room smelled very peculiar, not something Ayaan was comfortable with. He saw a ton of garbage on the desk, burger and chocolate wrappers and cocoa-cola cans. Probably the reason for the smell.

After several minutes had passed, commissioner Vishnu looked up to Ayaan. He was still waiting. He turned his computer to Ayaan.

"Should I buy the x-313 or z-513"

Ayaan sat upright from his chair and looked at the computer screen. The screen displayed a website which sold safes and vaults. There were two safes that were highlighted on the page, the model names were the ones the commissioner had asked Ayaan to choose from.
After nearly a minute of staring at the screen, dumbfounded as to why he was being asked this pointless question Ayaan replied "I don't know sir, I can't decide"

"Hmm, I don't blame you, I can't decide either, you might be wondering what I was doing" the commissioner said after reading Ayaan's perplexed expression.

"Not at all sir" Ayaan said with a straight face. He was eager to know why he was summoned and get out of the place as soon as possible.

"Well I will tell you anyway"

Ayaan held back his exasperation.

"You see when you have achieved as much as I have achieved you have a lot of assets that need to be kept safe"

"You mean money sir" Ayaan tried to show some interest.

"This is going to be my fourth safe, I am running out of places to hide... I mean keep my assets safe"

Ayaan looked around the room again, his sight was stuck at a painting hung in the wall on his right.
Commissioner caught what Ayaan had seen

"You are smart my boy, if you were smarter you would keep that to yourself"

The painting was an oil painting that showed the symbols of all the major religions of the world. Green, yellow, orange and white symbols painted on a black oil canvas, it looked beautiful. But that wasn't the reason Ayaan was staring at it, the reason was its purpose in the commissioner's office. Commissioner Vishnu was not a person that believed in equality or even religion, he barely followed his own neither did he have a knack for appreciation of great art. Ayaans investigators eye had located one of the commissioner's greatest possession and the painting was protecting it from being visible to ordinary people. Ayaan took his gaze off the painting, he didn't care for what was inside the hidden safe and it was definitely not worth getting on the bad side of the commissioner.

"So what was it you wanted to talk about sir" Ayaan tried desperately to change the topic.

"Oh yes! I wanted to know how the case I assigned you was going"
A sense of defeat was discovered within.

"It's still on going, I have some leads" Ayaan lied

"You are not fooling anyone Shahi, I know the case, I saw it before I assigned it to you"
Ayaan looked up

"Then why did you assigned it to me"

"Well to be honest I thought if anyone could solve such a case it would be you and to be more honest I think this case was colossal waste of time, and you would be perfect for it"

"So you just assigned it to me because you had better things to do and you thought I didn't" Ayaan could feel his anger.

"Calm down my boy" he got up from the chair bent to down under the table and brought up two glasses and a whisky bottle.

"I was hoping that you could solve it"

"While knowing that it can't be solved" Ayaan interrupted.

"Yes" the commissioner replied sternly while pouring drinks in the two glasses.

Ayaan knew it, he knew it from the very start that it was a bad idea to take this case, now his intuitions had been proven right.

Commissioner Vishnu took one glass filled with whiskey and slid the other across the table to Ayaan. Ayaan didn't take it he looked right at his face. The commissioner looked back and his eyes widened.

"Oh yes of course!" He took back the glass

"I completely forgot, you are the wrong person to offer this drink to, well no worries more drink for me. I would offer you something else but I have nothing else to offer" he smiled.

Ayaan ignored that

"So what do you want me to do"

"Something I thought you should have done a long time ago, leave things that are beyond your power to rest"

Ayaans heart sank, he felt a flush of emotions. Discouragement and comfort, frustration and satisfaction.

"Allow me to explain this in a way you will probably understand" he took a sip of his drink and continued. "there are two types of people in this world, the criminals who get caught and the criminals who don't" he raised his left hand and pointed towards the painting on the wall.

"Now you have spent nearly your whole life getting criminals to justice, you liked doing things your way so much that you never even joined the police force of this city. Even though I offered it to you several times, you didn't listen to me then but do now. This case was never meant to be solved, the guy is a freak. A coke head, womanizing son of a bitch with cash and gold that he never gave to anyone? No wonder nobody cares he is dead"

Ayaan was listening intently

"But-"

"No buts Ayaan" Ayaan was cut off. "I know all about the case before I gave it to you, and this is all there is to know about this case, you have lived in this city your entire life, you know better than to moan the lives of those who are linked with the father. You might get yourself hurt again, you have a daughter to look after."

"So what is it you want me to do sir" Ayaan knew what he was supposed to do but he couldn't help but ask.

"Let it go Ayaan Shahi, this is a puzzle that was never meant to be solved"

Complacency was discovered within.

CHAPTER TWELVE

It had been 5 days since Ayaans meeting with the commissioner. It was a pleasant Sunday morning and Ayaan was seated on his sofa with a cup of tea in his hand, the clock read 11:15.

Ayaan took a sip of his hot tea, which wasn't as hot as Ayaan liked because it had been sitting out for too long. Ayaan had just come from a long and relaxing bath which was longer and even more relaxing than he intended. He looked through the glass doors that led to the balcony and saw the sunlight beam through into the room. The view from the apartment used to be of fields of grass a whole series of them. This was back when Ayaan had just bought the apartment, the builder had promised not to compromise the view, he planning to buy all the nearby land just so that he could keep the great view from the apartment intact. This was more than 10 years ago and at that point Ayaan believed him. But now he knew that it was all just talk. All the view which Ayaan admired had been blocked by massive structures. Nevertheless, this apartment was still very special to Ayaan, he wouldn't leave it for the world. He bought this apartment with Maya, their first house, this was home.

Today Ayaan had planned to meet Mrs. Gupta. This case, as Ayaan had first intended was to be delegated to Milan, but now since there was nothing on his plate, he decided to take it. A busy mind never wanders, a mind needs direction, without that it's lost and a lost mind is a vulnerable mind. Ayaan had experienced that state of mind before. Back when he had just lost his father, he was lost as well. It took him some time but he got on the right track and he never was lost again.

As he gazed outside his apartment he heard voices coming from Ayman's room. She and Preeti were together and Ayman was helping her prepare for her role in the play. Ayaan could see Ayman's excitement regarding the play, but he had to be firm with this situation, Ayman deserved better. Barsha had dropped Preeti off earlier in the morning; she had to go out of town for business. Barsha was an art dealer and also an organizer. She traded works of art and also helped organize exhibitions for artist who wanted recognition. She was really good at her job and Ayaan really admired her taste. Several of the paintings that hung on Ayaan's walls were of her selection. She would be back in a couple of days so Ayaan had offered to keep Preeti at his place. Ayman would have someone to play with and Ayaan didn't mind having more people at his place, the apartment seemed quite lonely at times.

It took Ayaan nearly half an hour to get his things in order and then he was off to meet his old client with a new case. A new story was beginning.

It had been a week since Ayaan had visited the commissioner's office and had the truth hit him square in the face, but he had made his peace with it now. However sleep still eluded him and whenever he did fall asleep his dreams were recurring, but that of course was a different matter altogether.

It has been two days since Ayaan had met Mrs. Gupta and taken a new case. He had already been paid heavily in advance for a case which was not too complicated. Ayaan had been following Mr. Gupta for two and nothing substantial had come up. He had followed him to the office then to a bar and then back home. He was an honest and hardworking man with a jealous and annoying wife. She had assigned Ayaan the same case for nearly the 10th time, Ayaan guessed, still there was no quit in that woman. She was adamant that her husband was up to something with another woman. Just like all the previous cases she had assigned Ayaan to, she didn't mention who she suspected her husband was involved with nor did she explain how she had got such a suspicion. And just like before she made Ayaan promise not to tell her husband about it and to keep her informed about her husband's movements at all times, and just like before Ayaan had obliged to everything she requested.

It had been 4 days and Ayaan was still strongly directed to follow Mr. Gupta. But now as each day passed, Ayaan was even more confident in believing that he was right about Mr. Gupta. He had started to take time out for himself. Every day from 12-5 Mr. Gupta stayed at his office working. So Ayaan took that time out to get back to his gym and work out. He had been long out of touch and it was time to get fit again. He realized how much he had missed the gym, it was one place where he could take out his aggression and get his thoughts in line. After two hours each day, Ayaan was back at Mr. Guptas tail. Tracking his every movement and informing Mrs. Gupta all about it. This story wasn't very interesting and it felt like it never would. Ayaan had a strong feeling that this time things would end just like it did all the

113

previous times, a week of stalking and tailing and nothing particularly substantial coming out of it. A colossal waste of time.

A week had passed and Ayaan was getting tired of the entire situation. He was feeling great physically, but his insomnia wasn't getting any better. The dreams were vivid and always there.

It was Monday afternoon and Ayaan was in his car outside Mr. Guptas office, waiting. His routine was getting tedious and it all seemed pointless. He was frequenting in nearby restaurants for lunch, there were several of them in the neighborhood. He took an half an hour lunch break every day.

He could have gone back to his place, but he didn't want to miss out if something did happen, of course now when Ayaan thought about it he could have taken a good nap as well. It was yesterday when Ayaan realized that he had wasted way too much time on this case. The waiter at the restaurant where he used to go for the past week didn't bother taking the order, instead he just put a plate of what he usually had. Sometimes you need someone from the outside to tell you to get your shit straight, Ayaan thought. But one thing seemed very clear that Mr. Gupta was a very busy man. He didn't take breaks, not even on weekends, somewhere deep down Ayaan did to a certain extent understand the reason for Mrs. Guptas suspicions.

However Ayaan had visited the inside of the office secretly to see what was going on. But it was nothing but business. So now Ayaan had to put his foot down, he had to take charge of the situation and act. He couldn't be suspicious about such an innocent and hardworking man. He decided to visit Mrs. Gupta at her house, but he couldn't visit her while Mr. Gupta was at the house to, luckily Ayaan knew exactly where he was and where he would be for the next couple of hours. He finished his lunch and the waiter like he did previously brought him his regular meal. He finished it quickly, started his car and headed down to Mrs. Gupta.

It took him 37 minutes to reach his destination, which included intense traffic jams, damaged roads and a rapid change in weather. The sky was getting grey, the wind colder and Ayaan was impatient. He parked his car right in front of the Gupta mansion. The house was named very aptly, but designed very poorly. The house was large surrounded by other large houses on the street.

Ayaan didn't have a keen eye for design or architecture, but he didn't particularly appreciate the house in front of him. The house had a black gate that gave way into a cream colored bungalow surrounded by dense foliage and the scent of freshly mowed grass and newly bloomed flowers. But the problem with the house was that instead of having the entrance in the front or even at the side the bungalow had the entrance at the very back of the house. That meant that you had to travel all the way back to reach the entrance of the house, pass through the living room the dining room and the master bedroom which were all exposed through glass windows.

Ayaan exited his car and crossed the street. He pushed the black gate and it creaked open. He breathed in the fresh air and looked at the sky. He saw it getting greyer by the minute, it looked like a storm was brewing. The fresh smell of flowers and grass was overpowered by the smell of wet sand and damp leaves. Ayaan went through the passage that led to the back and also to the front entrance. Form follows inconvenience. Ayaan made his way through the living room window which was wide open and the room was abandoned.

The living room gave a view to the stairs that led to the first floor and the kitchen, there was no one in sight. He passed through another window and peeked, the dining room was empty and everything seemed dead. He arrived at the last window before he turned right and headed to ring the bell. The last window wasn't wide open and the room wasn't empty. The curtains were drawn so Ayaan could witness what was going on inside the room. The window was located such it faced the cupboards lined up on the opposite wall, the entry to the room was on the right of the cupboards and the door was firmly locked and shut. To the left lay the dresser and the mirror through which Ayaan could see the huge bed in the room and on top of it lay two people, naked.

Ayaan took a step back, shocked and astonished. He couldn't feel his hands, his feet wobbled and his eyes felt like they would pop out. His entire career flashed before his eyes, blurry pictures became clearer and the senseless became sensible. His questions answered. Why did Mrs. Gupta pay him so much money for such a juvenile case? Why did she always want to know where Mr. Gupta was? Everything became clear in a second. She had to know where he was because she didn't intend to get caught cheating on her husband, everything was planned and Ayaan was a pawn.

He wanted to scream, do something spontaneous and immature, he wanted to call me Gupta and tell him everything he knew and how he was betrayed by his wife. He could get his cell phone and call him right away, but he couldn't feel his hands and the energy drained away from his body.

So with every breath he could muster and every ounce of energy he could gather, he ran.

He ran out through the passage and out the gate onto the road. He didn't get in his car or even glance if it was present or not, he ran, through the empty street under the grey sky. The grey had shades and so did Ayaans emotions. He couldn't stop his feet and somehow didn't want to, he wanted to see where he was going when he had nowhere to go.

He ran through walkways and busy roads, through traffic and cars. He ran like he was 12 again, light and fast tears running down his right cheek. He ran away from all the betrayal and hatred, he ran from hopes and dreams. He ran from justice and everything he had fought for. He ran from the tears and the pain. He ran from himself.

When the legs stopped, the time stopped and for a minute so did Ayaans thoughts.

He felt he had travelled back 25 years. He gazed at the small structure that stood in front of him. No stranger would have considered it important, but for most of his childhood, this was the world to him. It was mosque and a very small one, and it surely didn't look like one. The mosque was about 50 years old and it looked like that as well. It might have easily been a decade or even more since it had been renovated or even decorated. The cracks on the wall outside were big and evident. The gates to the entrance were rusted. Ayaan didn't go inside at first he examined the building gazing it endlessly. He had spent hours in this building learning and thinking, and now he was back so many years later. After few minutes Ayaans breath became normal again and he started walking. Next to the compound wall that belonged to the mosque was a small path that led to the playground. Ayaan decided to go there first.

The clouds were still grey and the sky was gloomy. The playground was deserted and Ayaan saw nothing but a couple of footballs lying around.

Ayaan could see himself, sitting on a rock when he was just a kid, alone and secluded. The young Ayaan looked on to the ground and the kids playing there. There were five kids playing football and no one bothered a glance at Ayaan. A kid in the purple shirt kicked the ball harder than he had intended and the ball rolled out of play towards Ayaan

"Hey Ayaan, pass the ball"

The young Ayaan didn't realize at first that someone called his name

"Ayaan are you deaf!"
Ayaan looked at the kid

"Pass me the ball" the kid finished

Ayaan got up and kicked the ball hard, harder than he should have. The ball hit the kid in the purple shirt square in the chest, the kid tumbled and fell. Ayaan giggled
The kid got up, furious and started making his way towards Ayaan. He was evidently older than Ayaan and bigger like all the kids in the playground that time.

"You punk I am going to knock you out" screamed the kid in the purple shirt.

But before he could get his hands on Ayaan, a kid in dressed in blue shirt stopped him.

"Let it go Salman, look at this guy he is pathetic."
Salman stopped

"Yeah my mother told me not to talk to him, said his father was an evil man"

"My father was a good man" screamed Ayaan
The other kids came as well

"Yeah my father said the same thing to me"

"Yeah so did my father"
All the kids were now talking

"Your father did some bad things with other bad people and that's why he died. My mother said it was actually a good thing your father passed away, at least the world is a better place now" Salman finished.

Ayaan saw his younger self clench his fists, he was livid and rightfully so. Ayaan knew what was going to happen now, he was going to defend his father unsuccessfully while the kids laugh and humiliate his father further more. It was a long time since Ayaan had thought about that incident and the place where he was brought those memories rushing back.

But something distracted Ayaan, a drop of water fell on his left cheek he looked up, the grey clouds had finally given in to their natural instinct and let it pour. Ayaan had to go back to the mosque and find shelter, and Ayaan did just that.

Just before he entered the mosque he glanced in the distant and he saw an old apartment that was once his home. Ayaan opened the door to the mosque and went in.

The building was just as damaged on the inside as it was on the outside. The roof was not a permanent roof but a shed

119

made of metal. The carpets placed on the floor for prayers were also damaged and had big holes in them. Ayaan heard thunder outside and he could hear rain falling heavily on the metal shed above. The clatter of rain drops on the shed were evidence of how heavy the rainfall actually was and Ayaan was thankful he made it in time.

But Ayaan wasn't here to observe the mosque or to save himself from getting wet, he was here for one purpose and one purpose only, to talk to a man. A man he had not seen for a long time, a man who was there for him when no one else was, a man Ayaan loved more than his own father and the only man who would have answers to everything Ayaan has been going through, the cases and the dreams and everything else that had him so restless.

After Ayaan had had his moment of a trip down memory lane, he saw across the room to see the man, imam Suleiman. His grey beard was visible from the distant, always well-trimmed and maintained. He wore thick glasses that were probably 30 years out of style and had the same pair for the major part of his whole life. Even in the latter half of 70 he walked as firmly as a man in his 40s. But he did not notice Ayaan, he was busy talking to someone else.

Ayaan looked around, he saw 7 people in the mosque, apart from him, imam Suleiman and the man he was talking too. Everyone was busy praying and Ayaan decided to do the same. It took Ayaan nearly 10 minutes to complete his prayers and when he gazed in front of him imam Suleiman was standing and looking right back at him. He smiled and Ayaan smiled back, he walked over to Ayaan and gave him a tight hug. It was a long hug, but rightfully so, they hadn't met each other for a long time. After the hug imam Suleiman kissed him on his forehead.

"Ayaan Shahi! It's been a long time since I have seen that noble face. Too busy trying to make this city a better place for people like me"

Ayaan gave a faint smile "I am not so sure about that"
Imam smiled

"Come we have a lot to talk about"

They went to one corner of the mosque and sat down on the carpet.

The light in this part of the mosque was much brighter, every other place in the building was very gloomy. This is where Ayaan got the chance to see the imam properly. His body might have been in good shape and nowhere near of a man in his 70s, but his face had aged quite much. He had wrinkles and his skin seemed older. However his smile never changed and never did his eyes. His glasses always had a crack on the right panel, and the crack was still present to this day. Something's never change. But behind that cracked frame were his green eyes that shone with wisdom.

Ayaan recalled all he knew about Imam Suleiman and why he was so special to him. Imam Suleiman wasn't like most of the imams of the city, unlike them he was highly educated in not only religious knowledge but also academia. Imam Suleiman had studied human psychology and done mastered in the too, this was after he was quit the national army. He had then gotten to doing a PhD in world history and at last studying his religion and becoming and imam. Ayaan always questioned his decision to become an imam, he could have been very successful in his life if he had chosen to pursue it, but every time Ayaan had brought up the question the answer was always the same.

"Life is short, so there is no point wasting time in taking the long road to find out it's the wrong road."

Indeed Imam Suleiman had pursued so many different career paths to find out which one he liked and after achieving so much he realized he was looking for something very different.

"Well the place still looks the same" Ayaan started the conversation
Imam nodded

Ayaan looked around, he could hear the rain falling on the roof faster and with more force. There were three buckets placed in different places in the mosque, it was evidently for the leakage in the roof. As Ayaan looked around little drops of water fell down from the roof and into the bucket.

"Why don't you ever renovate this place, it could look so much better"

Imam smiled. "This mosque is home to more people than any other mosque in the neighborhood, and there are many, you know why?"
Ayaan didn't answer

"Because it has sentimental value, these cracked walls and broken roofs all tell a story about the people who pray here day and night and no amount of air conditioning or renovation can change that. You would know, you have the same value for this place as the others do, probably even a little more and that is the reason you are her today isn't it."

Ayaan was taken aback by that, he was caught, he chose not to respond, just looked down to the ground.

"So tell me Ayaan Shahi, why are you here"

Ayaan somewhere deep down knew why, but he couldn't find an answer. All he knew was that this was the place his body brought him to, he was still searching for the perfect answer as to why. But Ayaan had to respond

"I don't know" said Ayaan softly

"Ayaan I have known you for the better part of your life, and the Ayaan I know doesn't believe in not knowing things, so I repeat my question, why are you here?"
Ayaan still did not have an answer.

"I don't know" Ayaan replied with a bit of irritation

"I have known you since you were a little boy, and I have been there in all the ups and downs in your life, so tell me why are you here?

"I don't know, why don't you believe me" Ayaan said this a little louder.

"Because I don't, why are you here, Ayaan?

"Because I am afraid!" Ayaan blurted out loudly.

Imam Suleiman grinned as if he had got the answer he enacted to hear.

"Of what?" He asked politely

Ayaan recollected everything that has happened to him in recent days, right from the phone called he had received from Milan about the murder of me Agarwal up until the case he had undertaken with Mr. Gupta and his wife. All the while Ayaan explained this imam Suleiman listened intently, without uttering a word. Ayaan also mentioned his insomnia and his dreams with his father whenever he fell asleep. The imam's expression was unreadable, if Ayaan knew any better he would have believed that imam Suleiman hadn't understood a word he had said, but Ayaan knew the man too well to know that that was not true. After he was done talking and explaining his story he sat quietly, eager to hear what Imam had to say.

Ayaan had to wait a while, imam Suleiman looked around as if searching for an answer and after some time he responded.

"How long have you been on this case" he asked politely
Ayaan knew that he was talking about the Agarwal case.

"5-6 days" Ayaan replied, confused at the question
Imam Suleiman took some more time, he seemed to be in some sort of a deep thought process.

"I remember this one incident from when you were a child" imam started.

"You came to me angry at the kids of the society teasing you. This was right after your father had been diagnosed with AIDS and everyone in the neighborhood knew about it now. Everybody talked about it behind your back, but the kids said it to your face what others thought about your father. I knew what you were going through at that point and I knew how angry you were do you remember what I told you that day?"
Ayaan recalled

"Don't grow up angry at people who put you down, grow up despite them putting you down." Ayaan recalled this

124

particular phrase repeated to him.

"Yes yes, I did say that but that's not what I am talking about." Imam said

"Then what is it"

"Even though it is hard to believe or hard to see there is justice in this world, justice for the ones who deserve it. God overlooks everything that happens on this planet and he is just, and sooner or later he will bring justice to people who deserve it, give it time."

Ayaan now remembered.

"But what has it got to do with my problem" Ayaan inquired

"Do you know what you said to me? Imam paused but continued not waiting for an answer, "you said to me that it doesn't matter if God is just or not, when I grow up I will make sure justice is provided not only to the people that deserve it but to people who demand it. I will be the law around this town"

Imam paused to let Ayaan absorb everything he had just said and then he continued.

"This was the moment that defined Ayaan Shahi's future, this was the goal and ambition that you held dearest and closest to your heart. You went into the police and then became a private investigator just so you could bring a little justice to this city that is decaying day by day."

"So what's your point"

"My point is the Ayaan I knew did not give up on a case after 5 days, it took him that long just to get his mind started."

"But this case was different, there was nothing to get started on, it was all a dead end"

"You must have missed a link" said imam Suleiman

"I did not miss any link" Ayaan retorted
There was silence for a while.

"In my studies of world history I got to study a lot about the Egyptian civilization and everything regarding a its people and culture" imam continued. "One thing I was thoroughly fascinated by was their belief of life after death and how the soul will eventually return to the body after some time."
Ayaan listened intently.

"The Egyptians used to weigh their kings heart against gold to see if he was worthy of being mummified, after a lot of research I found out according to Egyptian scholars what made the heart way more than the gold and what made it weigh less. Egyptian scholars were trying to determine the reason of a good heart and the reason they came up with is was the man's purpose in this world and whether or not he fulfilled it. Scholars concluded that the heart was purer and weighed more than the gold, which meant it was more meaningful to god just because the person had fulfilled his purpose on earth and deserved to be incarnated again."
Ayaan had goose bumps on his hands.

"Ayaan, son, there is a lot of negativity in this world. This world is filled with people that live their lives never trusting others or never having the courage to see the good in them. All we can truly do in the short life that we have here is to not let all that negativity corrupt our purpose in this world. Life is going to be very hard if you can't see all the positives around you. You have made your purpose to be the law in an unjust world, stay true and stay strong, the world needs people like you."

Ayaan was left stunned, motion less he sat staring at the floor with his eyes wide open, trying to understand everything that he had just heard.

Nothing was discovered within.

CHAPTER THIRTEEN

His hands were drenched in red. The liquid was thick and smelled weird, he looked at it as the liquid dried in his hands. His palms were redder than anything red he had ever seen. He saw the floor on which stood his stool on which he was seated. He had covered the floor with white sheets, so no stain would come to the tiles. The sheet was covered with drops of the red liquid, but that could be cleaned up later. He looked up at what he had done, the result of something he had planned to do for a long time. It was now done, finished, over. Did he feel a sense of accomplishment? Indeed, but he also felt a lot of regret.

At the age 24 Aarsh was done with his masterpiece of a painting. He was proud of what he had accomplished here but he did feel regret as to why he hadn't thought about it earlier. The red paint on the canvas was still fresh and damp, but it had already begun to mix with all the other colors in the background. His hands were damp as well, the red paint was sticky and moist.

He went to the basin and washed all the paint on his hands away. With his hands clean now, Aarsh picked up the canvas from the sides and admired it for a little while. The painting consisted of man colored in dark colors standing on a street looking up as in the front of him a series of skyscrapers lined up, all breaking and falling in some sort of way. When closely observed from the buildings there were people falling off, falling on to the ground. However the most intriguing part of the painting was the background, filled with warm and bright colors, the sun was rising from the bottom, while the moon was still visible above. Every good painting needs a good name and Aarsh knew that and he had already thought of name.

As he held the painting in his hands he murmured the name, "the fall of civilization". Just uttering the name brought a smile to his face, weeks of work had finally paid off, it was done and it was good.

For Aarsh painting had already been a hobby, right from his childhood he had been very fond of colors. Now 24, painting had become a job, he sold his paintings at auctions and exhibitions. He entered competition and had won quite few of them as well. But all this was just an excuse for him to keep painting.

Aarsh realized there was some paint on his right cheek that he hadn't washed off. He went into the bathroom and looked himself in the mirror. His jet black hair was ruffled and a mess, his face was clean shaven. He saw the paint on the cheek and put some water to wipe it out. Out in the distance sirens wailed, Aarsh looked at himself in the mirror, his eyes widened.

"Could it be? Has it finally arrived? The consequences of his decision?" Aarsh thought. The sirens were sounding closer, and Aarsh was shaking. It wasn't a sound of an ambulance, ambulances don't come in groups.

"Had they finally come for him" thoughts were rushing through Aarsh's mind.

He quickly got out of the bathroom and went to the living room. The living room was where the painting was kept. The

129

floor was covered with white sheet with spots of red paint splattered all over. Certainly not a good sign, if Aarsh was to win some sympathy. He folded the sheets swiftly and kept them in the storage. He could still hear the sirens in the distance, Aarsh was panicking. There was no other noise in the surroundings and that made the sound of the sirens even more evident.

He was getting more anxious by the minute. Then in his panic Aarsh realized something his father had taught him very well, meditation. Aarsh's father was always urging Aarsh to meditate in any situation, it calms the nerves, it calms the brain, it calms the spirit, that's what his father used to say. Without hesitation, Aarsh sat down, closed his eyes and began meditating. Breathe in, breath out. His paintings flashed before his eyes. Breathe in breathe out, colors, strips of colors mixing and matching.

Breathe in breathe out, his last painting auction. Breathe in breathe out, having drinks with his friends. Breathe in breathe out, his last birthday party. Breathe in breathe out, his last New Year's party. Breathe in breathe out, and the memory of a gun in his hand and bald man lying dead in a chair. Breathe in, breathe out, the doorbell rang twice.

Aarsh opened his eyes. It was time!

The big red front door of Aarsh's house was locked completely. Aarsh took some time opening the door and after the door was opened, he saw two men standing on the porch. One man was short and stout. Although he wasn't very short from Aarsh, as Aarsh himself wasn't very tall. The short man was wearing a jacket and jeans and looked like he was waiting for instructions from the other man standing beside him.

The second man was taller than Aarsh, but was of average height, decent build, had black hair and had a stubble that looked unintentional. He was wearing a blue shirt with black pants.

"Yes?" Aarsh asked politely.

"Ayaan Shahi, private investigator" the tall man in the blue shirt flashed his id in front of Aarsh rapidly. "And this is Milan, we are here to ask you a few questions regarding a case, are you Aarsh?"

"Yes" Aarsh replied

"Aarsh Agarwal?" The short man named Milan swooped in.

"Yes" Aarsh replied again

"Would you mind if we come in" Ayaan asked politely.

"Sure" Aarsh responded calmly.

After nearly 5 minutes all three people were seated on the sofa and Aarsh had already offered some beverage but both men had refused.

Aarsh was nervous, scared even, but he knew what he had to say and he tried to calm himself down and project some confidence. The private investigator who called himself Ayaan Shahi and his assistant Milan were seated on the sofa, while Aarsh was seated on the opposite side of it. Aarsh was fidgeting with his fingers and was evidently more nervous than he tried to portray. And Aarsh believed Ayaan picked up on that.

After taking a deep breath, Ayaan started to speak.

"We are here to investigate a murder of a man called -"

"Mr. Agarwal" Aarsh interrupted.

"Yes how you did-"

"I know about your case and the murder of a man that nobody really knows?" Aarsh interrupted again.

"Yes!" Ayaan said, he seemed more interested and so did his partner. Aarsh was feeling confident as well.

"Because I killed him, I am the murderer" Aarsh said almost sounding proud.
Both men exchanged puzzled looks.

"Why did you kill him, you are his son right?" Milan asked before Ayaan could say anything, excitement and curiosity had taken over both men and it was evident on their face.

"What makes you think I am his son?" Aarsh asked.
Both men exchanged another puzzled look

"Because your last name is Agarwal so we assumed that -"

"I was his son?" Aarsh interrupted Ayaan again

"Yes!" Ayaan replied

"Things don't always seem to be what they are so they Ayaan Shahi?"
Ayaan had frown on his face trying to contemplate what

Aarsh was saying.

"Some people that seem so bad turn out to be good instead and some people who you think you have never seen have actually met you" Aarsh finished

"What do you mean" Ayaan asked, confused.

"I actually have met you, I saw you at the police station, when you went to meet the commissioner"

Aarsh witnessed Ayaans eyes widening, he surely realized it now. He had bumped into Ayaan in the station.

"You were the guy with a handful of documents that flew away when I bumped into you" Ayaan realized
Aarsh gave a faint nod.

"Why were you at the police station?"

"I went there with the intention to confess the murder with proof"

"Then why didn't you?" Ayaan asked quickly.

"Because I bumped into you and that changed everything. You see prior to me going to the police station, I had gotten the impression that this case had gone unnoticed. I mean there was no news on the television or the paper And I felt confessing to the murder might give it the recognition I wanted. But when I bumped into you and heard why you were there I felt that there was at least one man who cares and one man who will do this case justice"

Ayaan lowered his gaze, Aarsh didn't know the man very well

but he could fell as of Ayaan was ashamed of something.

"Why did you want this case to be recognized so badly" Milan asked the question.

"To pay back for everything Mr. Agarwal did for me"

"By killing him?" Milan added

Aarsh took a deep breath, he had been preparing for this moment for a long time.

"Mr. Agarwal was not my father, but he was the closest thing to a father I ever had. Frankly speaking I don't even know who my father is to this day. Many years back my mother used to work as his assistant and I was very young. We were in dire need for money and he gave it to us, he paid for both me and my sister's education and made us capable of what we are today. He never had any family, but we were as good as family to him. Even though he had no relation to us before, he helped us become who we are today and I do not care what you have heard about him, but he was an angel"

"And you killed that Angel" Milan said
Ayaan was listening intently with his eyes still locked on the floor.

"He was gonna die either way"

"What?" Milan questioned

"He had cancer" Ayaan said, before Aarsh could clarify the exact same thing.

"Final stage, Dr. Anand's report came in" Ayaan said, looking at Aarsh now.

"But but but why kill him then, cut his life short" Milan was confused

"How many movies, songs or sport events have you watched again just because the people involved in it are no longer in this world and you just heard about their death in the news. Think about it, a person you did not know or care about on a personal level could have such an impact on you after their death. Sometimes all people need to do is die to get back the recognition they deserve, it's twisted but that's how the world works. You wouldn't care as much for an artist who is alive and well as much as you would about him after he is dead. Death is a powerful tool, murder is a weapon. Just think about all you have learnt about Mr. Agarwal as person, I am sure it is not very nice, would anyone give a rat's ass whether Mr. Agarwal loves or died? But suddenly there is a murder and everybody wants to know who did it. Information is power in the world we live in today and all humans want it." Aarsh finished.

"But what about all cocaine he bought and his relationships with his secretary?. I visited his apartment and I saw all the cocaine stashed in the corner, so I know it's not a rumor"
Ayaan asked after patiently forming the question in his head.
Aarsh laughed, a sarcastic laughter.

"I thought you might have understood the whole situation from the story I put in Mr. Agarwal's coat"

"The pious, drunkard and fornicator?" Ayaan questioned

135

"That's the one, if you had understood the intention of that story, this story would have been a lot shorter"

Aarsh paused, looking at both faces eager to hear more.

"Mr. Agarwal, my father was an odd man. I say this because he cared a lot about people and not only people he knew, but everyone in general. The only reason he bought all the cocaine was just so no one else would and the secretary is actually my sister, he hired her to help us out some more. I can't tell you how much you misjudged my father, I think you can do that better than me, all I can say is that he was the best man I have ever met"

Aarsh saw both men exchange nervous looks, they looked ashamed even.

"So let me ask you this Mr. Shahi have you ever cared, while not being cared for, have you ever loved but not loved back? If no, then for the very first time in your life you have known a person whose priority was to trade smiles for a life of loneliness and solitude"

The room went silent for a while, as all three men sat quietly contemplating everything they had discussed here. Aarsh was getting nervous again, all the confidence he had was used up. He felt like he was going to prison, he knew he was going to prison, it was just about time. Ayaan asked for a glass of water and Aarsh gave it to him. After drinking Ayaan got up from the sofa.

"You know as a private investigator, I don't have the authority to arrest anyone. My job is to report it to the officials and then they take action. The way I see here, this was a pleasant conversation between two strangers getting to know each other over a glass of water and that's all"

A smile formed on Aarsh's face, he could feel it. Tears were forming in his eyes, he could feel them too.

Ayaan went in for a handshake before he left, but Aarsh hugged him tight.

"Thank you Mister Shahi, it takes great love to forgive someone, to live with the guilt, regret and pain and you right here are the most loving of them all."

And seconds later the door shut and both men were out the door and Aarsh went back to his painting he looked at it intently for a while and then he turned it upside down. He smiled as he looked on and whispered the final name of the painting "the rise of hope"

CHAPTER FOURTEEN

The walk back to the car was long, the house he had just came out of was located in the midst of a very narrow street. Ayaan had parked his car in the front of the gate that led to the narrow street. Ayaan walked ahead and Milan walked right behind him. The weather was pleasant, the clouds had cleared, and the night was filled with stars. Evidence of that there was heavy rainfall still remained prominent through the puddles on the street and the wet roads. The air was cool and calm and in the middle of all of that was Ayaan whose heart was beating fast and so were his legs. Not too long after Ayaan reached his car, it was parked on the side of the road and the road was empty. No sign of life whatsoever.

The whole way Ayaan didn't speak a word and neither did Milan.

Ayaans mind was racing, he was emotional. So instead of getting in the car and driving home, Ayaan sat on the footpath right next to his car. Milan joined.

They sat silently for some time, they just looked blankly at the road and the sky.

After a while Ayaan reached out his hand into Milan's shirt pocket and grabbed the pack of cigarettes. He took one out lit it and smoked it.

"Is everything alright sir" Milan asked calmly as he saw his boss puffing smoke into the sky.

Ayaan could feel his heart sink a little, it was definitely heavier, and it seemed like he couldn't bear the weight because his eyes started to water.

"I know what my dad meant now, and he was right"

Seeing the perplexed expression on Milan's face Ayaan continued. "For some time now I have been having these dreams about my dad, who would come in to my dreams and ask me to discover what's within. Till now I didn't know what he meant but now I do, now I know so well"

Ayaan grabbed another cigarette and lit it up.

"I always thought it was something of a feeling that I haven't discovered, or a part of me that was to be found, but the fact is it was me, I was missing and I had to discover myself, my purpose and do justice to it. I believe that when someone loses faith in himself and what he is doing, he loses the ability to trust, to believe, to forgive, he loses his ability to love. And for so long I have been lost and I never knew."

Tears fell from his eyes as Milan listened intently.

"It took a stranger with no name and no identity to tell me who I am. Do some people actually go through life never knowing who they really are, do they go through their whole life never knowing their potential for good?"

Milan realized he had to answer
"Well I can't say about everyone but you are not one of them sir"

"You think?"

"Yes I do, it takes great courage to hope when you are feeling hopeless, and you did that. Even though you blame yourself for not coming through first, you did come through eventually. You can go home tonight knowing that you made sure that a hero didn't die as a villain."

Ayaan nodded "You are right, he was a hero and he deserves that recognition. Call in the media tomorrow and tell them everything that we know. I want him all over the news in the city, everybody should know who he was"

"Sir, but we still don't know his first name, what should we do about that?"

Ayaan smiled, "it doesn't matter, the beauty lies in the work, not the name"

Milan nodded in agreement.

That was the thing with Milan that Ayaan admired so much, it didn't matter if he understood everything Ayaan said but he always listened. And somehow by talking to him Ayaan always felt lighter and better.

"Marlboro's? I feel like I am paying you way too much" Ayaan said jokingly looking at the burning cigarette.

They both laughed, Ayaan felt like he hadn't laughed in so long, it was a good feeling.

After that both parted ways, Ayaan sat in his car and started driving back home. The entire road back was wet but the sky was still clear as a summer night. It wasn't long until

Ayaan reached home, he parked his car in his parking spot and made his way inside the building. The elevator wasn't working once more, so Ayaan made his way to the staircase.

Instead of finding the staircase deserted as he expected it to be he saw Barsha sitting at the bottom stair. With her heels in her hands she sat wearing a blue dress.

Ayaan didn't say anything, but just sat down next to her.

"I broke my heels" she said, knowing Ayaan was listening. Ayaan saw the broken heel in her hands.

"And I am little drunk" she giggled slurring a little bit Ayaan smiled, he understood that very well.

She turned to Ayaan looking at him directly. "What were you doing out?"

"I solved the case, the mystery is solved"

"You are the mystery Ayaan Shahi" she kissed him on his cheek, put her head on his shoulder and held his hand.

They say there for a while in silence.

Ayaan reached a deserted apartment when he opened the door to his house. Everyone was asleep, the dim lights in the apartment led the way through to Ayaans bed room. But before he made his way to the bed room he sat down on the dining table. The table was empty, except for the basket of fruits that lay in the middle. But just under the basket lay a piece of paper, the basket made sure that the paper didn't fly away. Ayaan grabbed the piece of paper and unfolded it. It was the same paper Ayaan had refused to sign some time ago. The approval letter for Ayman's play. Ayaan looked at the paper for a while, took a pen and signed it. It was time to lose some control, stop thinking as much and let go of some things that he doesn't understand. Because in the end it will all make sense, Ayaan was just too close to see the big picture.

He kept the paper on the table and headed to his room. He changed his clothes, said his prayers and went to bed. He lay in bed thinking about the case and everything that had transpired in recent days. And after a while he cleared his head of everything and shut his eyes. And he slept, because now his mind was free of thoughts, free of expectations and decisions. And he knew that he wouldn't dream because everything that he needed to know for now, he had learned. So he slept, slowly letting go of control, his body became motionless and free. For now he knew that there are only two kinds of people in the world, the ones who believe and the ones who don't. He thought about the poem he read in Mr. Agarwal's apartment, the words circles in his head as he slowly slipped into the world in his head, the world of the unknown and embraced it, because tomorrow is just another chapter in his story.

EPILOGUE

POEM BY MR. AGARWAL

In my dying days I have something I would like to confess
This is something I want everyone to know something I want
to press

I have travelled and seen the world all-around
I have been successful and with money and luxury is what I
surround

But nothing fascinates me as much as people do
Nothing makes me wonder more than the actions the people
around me pursue

I have seen them love and lose it
I have seen them say petty things and actually believe it

I have known them to fight over beliefs and virtues
Seen them kill and torture others over different values

No thought horrifies me more than the sight of depleting
humanity
And the insane degradation of sanity

143

With my last breath I hope for more love and compassion
And I believe everyone to find their own passion

I know it is tough to be someone else than what people want
you to be
But in end it all makes sense trust me

I have seen lives end thinking of the world as a playground
and life as a game
And every second of my dying minutes I thank god that I
was never the same.

It's almost funny to think about how much we have lived and
how little we know about living

ABOUT THE AUTHOR

Zaid Maniar is an architectural student with a passion for writing. Residing in Ahmedabad, Zaid studied in Mahatma Gandhi International School (MGIS) and has been a huge fan of literature and its works. Greatly influenced by writers like Samuel Beckett and Oscar Wilde, these influences are very prominent in Zaid's works.